MILLS & BOON®

is delighted to present
popular author
SARA CRAVEN'S
60th novel:
Rome's Revenge

Congratulations, Sara!

Sara Craven was born in South Devon, and grew up surrounded by books in a house by the sea. After leaving grammar school she worked as a local journalist, covering everything from flower shows to murders. She started writing for Mills & Boon® in 1975. Apart from writing, her passions include films, music, cooking and eating in good restaurants. She now lives in Somerset.

Sara Craven has appeared as a contestant on the Channel Four game show *Fifteen to One* and is also last ever winner of the 1997 *Mastermind of Great Britain* championship.

Recent titles by the same author:

THE TYCOON'S MISTRESS

ROME'S REVENGE

BY
SARA CRAVEN

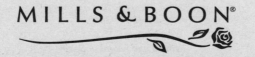

First published in Great Britain 2001
Harlequin Mills & Boon Limited,
Eton House, 18-24 Paradise Road, Richmond, Surrey TW9 1SR

© Sara Craven 2001

ISBN 0 263 82539 6

Set in Times Roman 10½ on 11¾ pt.
01-1001-47660

Printed and bound in Spain
by Litografía Rosés, S.A., Barcelona

CHAPTER ONE

THE charity ball was already in full swing when he arrived.

Rome d'Angelo traversed the splendid marble foyer of the large Park Lane hotel and walked purposefully through the massive archway which led to the ballroom. A security man considered asking for his ticket, took a look at the dark, uncompromising face and decided against it.

Inside the ballroom, Rome halted, frowning a little at the noise of the music and the babble of laughter and chat which almost drowned it. In his mind's eye he was seeing a hillside crowded with serried rows of vines, and a hawk hovering silently against a cloudless sky, all enshrouded in a silence that was almost tangible.

Coming here tonight was a mistake, and he knew it, but what choice did he have? he asked himself bitterly. He was gambling with his future, something he'd thought was behind him for ever. But of course he'd reckoned without his grandfather.

He accepted a glass of champagne from a passing waiter, and moved without haste to the edge of the balcony, which overlooked the ballroom floor. If he was aware of the curious glances which pursued him, he ignored them. By this time he was used to attracting attention, not all of it welcome. He'd soon learned in adolescence the effect that his six-foot-three, lean, muscular body could generate.

At first he'd been embarrassed when women had eyed him quite openly, using his broad-shouldered, narrow-hipped frame to fuel their private fantasies. Now he was simply amused, or, more often, bored.

But his attention tonight was focused on the several hundred people gyrating more or less in time with the music below him, his frowning gaze scanning them closely.

He saw the girl almost at once. She was standing at the edge of the dance floor, dressed in a silver sheath which lent no grace to a body that was on the thin side of slender and made her pale skin look tired and washed out. Like a shinny ghost, he thought critically. Yet she'd probably dieted herself into that condition, boasting about the single lettuce leaf she allowed herself for lunch.

Why the hell couldn't she be a woman who at least looked like a woman? he wondered with distaste. And how was it, with all her money, no one had ever shown her how to dress?

For the rest, her shoulder-length light brown hair was cut in a feathered bob, and, apart from a wristwatch, she seemed to be wearing no jewellery, so she didn't flaunt her family's money.

She was very still, and quietly, almost fiercely alone, as if a chalk circle had been drawn round her which no one was permitted to cross. Yet he could not believe she was here unescorted.

The Ice Maiden indeed, he thought, his lips twisting with wry contempt, and definitely not his type.

He'd met them before, these girls who, cushioned by their family's riches, could afford to stand aloof and treat the rest of the world with disdain.

And one of them he'd known well.

His frown returned.

It was a long time since he'd thought about Graziella. She belonged strictly to his past, yet she was suddenly back in his mind now.

Because, like the girl below him, she was someone who'd had it made from the day she was born. Who didn't have to be beautiful or beguiling, which she was, or even civil, which she'd never been, because her place in life was preordained, and she didn't have to try.

And that was why Cory Grant, in turn, could stand there, in her expensive, unbecoming gown, daring the world to keep its distance.

Dangerous things—dares, he thought, his firm mouth twisting.

Because the challenge implicit in every line of her rigid figure was making him wonder just what it would take to melt that frozen calm.

Then a slight movement focused his gaze more closely, and he realised that her hands were clenching and unclenching in the folds of the silver dress.

He thought, Ah—so there's a chink in the lady's armour, after all. Interesting.

And right on cue, as if she was suddenly conscious that she was being watched, she looked up at the balcony and her eyes met his.

Rome deliberately let his gaze hold hers for a long count of three, then he smiled, raised his champagne glass in a silent toast and drank to her.

Even across the space that separated them he could see the sudden burn of colour in her face, then she turned and walked away, heading for the archway which led to the cocktail bar.

If I was still gambling, he thought, what odds would I give that she'll look round before she gets to the bar?

It seemed at first he'd have lost his money, but then, as she reached the entrance, he saw her hesitate and throw a swift glance over her shoulder, aimed at where he was standing.

The next second she was gone, swallowed up by the crowd inside the bar.

Rome grinned to himself, then drank the rest of his champagne, setting the empty glass down on the balustrade.

He took his mobile phone from the pocket of his tuxedo and dialled a number.

When his call was answered, he said, his voice cool and abrupt, 'I've seen her. I'll do it.'

He rang off, and went back the way he'd come, his long, lithe stride carrying him across the foyer and out into the chill darkness of the night.

Cory hadn't wanted to come to the ball. And particularly she hadn't wanted to come with Philip, who, she guessed, had been set up by her grandfather to bring her.

She thought, I really wish he wouldn't do that, but her inner smile was tender. She knew that Arnold Grant only wanted the best for her. The problem was they'd never agree on what that 'best' was.

In Arnold's view it was a husband, wealthy, steady and suitable, who would provide her with a splendid home and, in due course, babies.

For Cory it was a career, not even remotely connected with Grant Industries, and total independence.

Currently, she drew an over-generous salary as Arnold's personal assistant, which meant that she organised his diary, made sure his domestic life ran smoothly, and acted as his hostess and companion at social events.

She felt a total fraud, knowing full well that all those activities could have fitted easily into her spare time, enabling her to do a job where she earned the money she was paid.

But Arnold insisted that he could not do without her, and had no hesitation in playing the old and frail card if he sensed she was near to rebellion.

Being allowed to move out of the big family house in

Chelsea and rent a modest flat of her own had been a major concession it had taken her nearly a year of argument and cajolery to win.

'How can you think of leaving?' he'd protested pitifully. 'You're all I've got. I thought you'd be here with me for the few years I have left.'

'Gramps, you're a monster.' Cory had hugged him. 'You're going to live for ever, and you know it.'

But although she no longer lived under his roof, he still felt he had *carte blanche* to meddle in her affairs.

And this evening was a case in point. He was a major contributor to the charity in question, and she was there to represent him, accompanied by a man who'd probably been blackmailed into bringing her.

Not, she decided, a pretty thought.

And so far it was all pretty much the disaster she'd expected. She and her escort had barely exchanged half a dozen words, and she'd seen the fleeting expression on his face when she'd emerged from the cloakroom.

You think this dress is bad? She'd wanted to say. You should have seen the ones I turned down. And I only bought it because I was running out of time and desperate, although I recognise a giant sack which also covered my face would have been a better choice.

But of course she'd said nothing of the kind. Just steadied her sinking heart and allowed him to take her into the ballroom.

And when Philip had dutifully asked her to dance with him she'd rewarded him by stepping on his foot. A painful process when your shoes were size sevens.

After which he'd hastily offered to get her a drink, and disappeared into the bar. That had been almost fifteen minutes ago, and it was more than time she went to look for him.

For all he knew, she thought, she could be lying on the floor, her face blackened and her tongue swollen with thirst.

She sighed under her breath. She always felt such a fool at these events. Such a fish out of water. For one thing, at five foot nine she was taller than most of the women. She was almost taller than Philip, which was another nail in the evening's coffin. Thank God she'd worn low heels.

She was a lousy dancer, too, she acknowledged with detachment. She had no natural rhythm—or even basic coordination, if it came to that. If she could find no one else's feet, she would fall over her own instead.

And she could usually manage a maximum of two minutes' bright social chatter, before her brain went numb and her pinned-on smile began to hurt.

At this moment she could only think how much she'd rather be at home, curled up with a book and a glass of good wine.

But now she really ought to move, before people thought she'd been actually glued to the spot, and make an attempt to find her unfortunate escort.

Maybe she could plead a sudden migraine and let him off the hook altogether, she thought.

She wasn't sure when she first became aware that someone was watching her.

Probably wondering if it was just the dress, or whether she'd genuinely been turned into a pillar of salt, she thought, glancing indifferently upwards.

And paused, conscious that her heart had given a sudden, unexpected lurch.

Because this was not the sort of man to give her even a passing look under normal circumstances.

And as their eyes met, some warning antenna began to send out frantic messages, screaming *Danger*.

He was immaculately dressed in conventional evening

clothes, but a bandanna around his unruly mane of curling dark hair and a black patch over one eye would have suited him better.

Although that was utter nonsense, she castigated herself. He was probably a perfectly respectable lawyer or accountant. Certainly no buccaneer could afford the arm and leg tonight's tickets had cost.

And it was time she stopped goggling like an idiot and beat a dignified retreat.

But, before she could move, he smiled and lifted the glass he was holding in a silent toast.

Cory could feel one of the agonising blushes that were the bane of her life travelling up from her toes.

All she had to do was turn her head and she would find the real recipient of all this attention standing behind her, she thought. Someone blonde and gorgeous, who knew how to wear clothes and probably how to take them off as well. Someone who could make a remark about the weather sound like an explicit sexual invitation.

I'm just in the way, she told herself.

But there was no one standing behind her. There was herself. And he was looking at her, and only her, smiling, as if he was watching. Waiting for her to do something.

Cory felt a sudden drop of sweat slide between her breasts like ice on her heated skin. Was aware of a swift flurry in her breathing.

Because she wanted to go to him. She wanted almost desperately to walk across the ballroom and up those wide marble stairs to where he was standing.

But, even more potently, she wanted him to come to her instead, and the swift, unexpected violence of that need jolted her out of her unwelcome trance and back to reality.

She thought, My God—this is crazy. And, more determinedly, I've got to get out of here—now...

She wheeled, and walked swiftly towards the cocktail bar and the errant Philip.

She risked a quick look over her shoulder and realised with mingled alarm and excitement that he was still there, still watching her, and still smiling.

My God, she thought again shakily. Philip might not be very exciting, or even marginally attentive, but at least he doesn't look like a pirate on his night off.

She looked round the crowded bar and eventually spotted him, sitting at a corner table with a bunch of his cronies, and roaring with laughter.

It was paranoid to think she might be the subject of the joke. Indeed, all the evidence suggested that he'd completely forgotten about her.

So—I'm paranoid, she thought with a small mental shrug. But once bitten...

At the bar, she asked for a white wine spritzer, and was just about to take her first sip when someone touched her shoulder.

She started violently, sending half the contents of her glass sloshing over the hated silver dress, and turned, half in hope, half in dread.

'Cory?' It was Shelley Bennet, an old schoolfriend, who now worked full time for the charity. 'I've been looking all over the place for you. I'd begun to think you'd chickened out.'

Cory sighed, mopping at herself with a minute lace hanky. 'No such luck. Gramps was adamant.'

'But surely you haven't come on your own?' Shelley's frown was concerned.

'My partner's over there, taking a well-deserved break,' Cory said drily. 'I may have broken his toe.' She hesitated. 'Shelley, when you were in the ballroom just now, did you notice a man?'

'Dozens,' Shelley said promptly. 'They tended to be dancing with women in long frocks. Strange behaviour at a ball, don't you think?'

'Well, this one seemed to be on his own. And he didn't look as if dancing was a major priority.'

Ravishment, maybe, she thought, and looting, with a spot of pillage thrown in.

Shelley's eyes glinted. 'You interest me strangely. Where did you see him?'

'He was up on the balcony.' Cory gave a slight frown. 'Usually you know exactly who's going to be at this kind of occasion, yet he was a total stranger. I've never seen him before.'

'Well, he seems to have made quite an impression,' Shelley said with affectionate amusement. 'You look marginally human for a change, my lamb, rather than as if you'd been carved out of stone.'

'Don't be silly,' Cory said with dignity.

Shelley's eyes danced. 'How much to look down the guest list and supply you with a name, if not a phone number?'

'It's not like that,' Cory protested. 'It's just such a novelty to see a new face at these things.'

'I can't argue with that.' Shelley gave her a shrewd look. 'Was it a nice new face?'

'No, I can't say that. Not *nice*, precisely.' Cory shook her head. *Not 'nice' at all.* 'But—interesting.'

'In that case I shall definitely be reviewing the guest list.' Shelley slipped an arm through her friend's. 'Come on, love. Point him out to me.'

But the tall stranger had vanished. And, but for the empty champagne glass on the balustrade in front of where he'd been standing, Cory would have decided he was simply a figment of her imagination.

'Snapped up by some predatory woman, I expect,' Shelley said with a sigh. 'Unless he took a good look at the evening's entertainment potential and decided that charity begins at home.'

Actually, he was taking a good look at me, Cory thought, rather forlornly. And probably writing me off as some sad, needy reject.

Aloud, she said briskly, 'Not a bad idea, either.'

She hailed a lurking waiter, and wrote a brief note of excuse to Philip on his order pad. 'Would you see that Mr Hamilton gets this, please? He's at the corner table in the cocktail bar.'

Shelley regarded her darkly. 'Are you running out on me, too—friend?'

''Fraid so,' Cory told her cheerfully. 'I've put in an appearance, so my duty's done and Gramps will be mollified.'

'Until the next time,' Shelley added drily. She paused. 'And what about your escort?'

'He's done his duty, too.' Cory smiled reassuringly. 'And I'd hate to have to fight off a token pass on the way home.'

'Maybe it wouldn't be token,' said Shelley. She was silent for a moment. 'Love, you aren't still tied up over that prat Rob, are you? You haven't let him ruin things for anyone else you might meet?'

'I never give him a thought,' Cory said, resisting an impulse to cross her fingers. 'And even if I believed in Mr Right, I can tell you now that Philip doesn't measure up.'

Shelley's eyes gleamed. 'Then why not opt for some good, unclean fun with Mr Wrong?'

For a brief moment Cory remembered a raised glass, and a slanting smile, and felt her heart thump all over again.

She said lightly, 'Not really my scene. The single life is safer.'

Shelley sighed. 'If not positively dull. Well, go home, if

you must. I'll ring you tomorrow and we'll fix up supper and a movie. The new Nicolas Cage looks good.'

'I had no real objection to the old Nicholas Cage,' said Cory. She gave Shelley a brief kiss on the cheek, and went.

The cab driver was the uncommunicative sort, which suited Cory perfectly.

She sat in the corner of the seat, feeling the tensions of the evening slowly seeping away.

She needed to be much firmer with Gramps, she told herself. Stop him arranging these dates from hell for her. Because she'd laughed off Philip's bad manners, and ducked the situation, that didn't mean she hadn't found the whole thing hurtful.

He'd left her standing around looking stupid, and vulnerable to patronage by some stranger who thought he was Mr Charm.

A hanging offence in more enlightened times, she told herself, as she paid off the cab and went into her building.

One disadvantage of living alone was having no one to discuss the evening with, she thought wryly, as she hung her coat in the wardrobe.

She could always telephone her mother, currently pursuing merry widowhood in Miami, but she'd probably find Sonia absorbed in her daily bridge game. And Gramps would only want to hear that she'd had a good time, so she'd have to fabricate something before she saw him next.

Maybe I'll get a cat, she thought. The final affirmation of spinsterhood. Which at twenty-three was ridiculous.

Perhaps I should change my name to Tina, she thought. There Is No Alternative.

She carefully removed the silver dress, and placed it over a chair. She'd have it cleaned, she decided, and send it to tonight's charity's second-hand shop. It would do more good there than it had while she'd been wearing it. Or had it really been wearing her?

Moot point, she thought, reaching for her moss-green velvet robe. And paused...

She rarely looked at herself in the mirror, except when she washed her face or brushed her hair, but now she found she was subjecting herself to a prolonged and critical scrutiny.

The silver-grey silk and lace undies she wore concealed very little from her searching gaze, so no false comfort there.

Her breasts were high and firm, but too small, she thought disparagingly. Everywhere else she was as flat as a board. At least her legs were long, but there were deep hollows at the base of her neck, and her shoulderblades could slice bread.

No wonder her blonde, glamorous mother, whose finely honed figure was unashamedly female, had tended to view her as if she'd given birth to a giraffe.

I'm just like Dad and Gramps, she acknowledged with a sigh. And if I'd only been a boy I'd have been glad of it.

She put on her robe and zipped it up, welcoming its warm embrace.

She dabbed cleanser on to her face, and tissued away the small amount of make-up which was all she ever wore. A touch of shadow on her lids, a glow of pink or coral on her soft mouth, and a coat of brown mascara to emphasise the curling length of the lashes that shaded her hazel eyes. Her cheekbones required no accenting.

From the neck up she wasn't too bad, she thought judiciously. It was a shame she couldn't float round as a disembodied head.

But she couldn't understand why she was going in for this kind of personal assessment anyway. Unless it was

Shelley's reference to Rob, and all the unhappy memories his name still had the power to evoke.

Which is really stupid, she thought quickly. I should put it behind me. Move on. Isn't that what we're always being told?

But some things weren't so easy to leave behind.

She went across her living room into her small galley-kitchen and poured milk into a pan, setting it on the hob to heat. Hot chocolate was what she needed. Comfort in a mug. Not a stony trip down memory lane.

When her drink was ready, she lit the gas fire and curled up in her big armchair, her hands cupped round the beaker, her gaze fixed on the small blue flames leaping above the mock coals.

One day, she thought, she'd have a huge log fire in a hearth big enough to roast an ox.

In fact, if she wanted, she could have one next week. One word to Gramps, and mansions with suitable fireplaces would be laid open for her inspection.

Only, she didn't want.

She'd found out quite early in life that as the sole heiress to the Grant building empire the word was hers for the asking. That her grandfather was ready to gratify any whim she expressed. Which was why she'd learned to guard every word, and ask for as little as possible.

And this flat, with its one bedroom and tiny bathroom, was quite adequate for her present needs, she thought, looking round her with quiet satisfaction.

The property company who owned it had raised no objection to her getting rid of the elderly fitted carpets and having the floorboards sanded and polished to a gleaming honey shine.

She'd painted the walls a deep rich cream, and bought a

big, comfortable sofa and matching chair covered in a corded olive-green fabric.

She'd made a dining area, with a round, glass-topped table supported by a cream pedestal and a pair of slender high-backed chairs, and created an office space with a neat corner desk which she'd assembled herself from a pack during one long, fraught evening, and which held her laptop, her phone and a fax machine.

Not that she worked at home a great deal. She'd been determined from the first that the flat would be her sanctuary, and that she would leave Grant Industries behind each time she closed her door.

Although she could never really be free of it for long, she acknowledged with a smothered sigh.

But she used her home computer mainly to follow share dealings on the Internet—an interest she'd acquired during her time with Rob, and the only one to survive their traumatic break-up. A hobby, she thought, that she could pursue alone.

It had never been her parents' intention for her to be an only child. Cory had been born two years after their marriage, and it had been expected that other babies would follow in due course.

But there had seemed no real hurry. Ian and Sonia Grant had liked to live in the fast lane, and their partying had been legendary. Sonia had been a professional tennis player in her single days, and Ian's passion, apart from his wife and baby, had been rally driving.

Sonia had been playing in an invitation tournament in California when a burst tyre had caused Ian's car to spin off a forest road and crash, killing him instantly.

Sonia had tried to assuage her grief by re-embarking on the tennis circuit, and for a few years Cory had travelled

with her mother in a regime of constantly changing nannies
and hotel suites.

Arnold Grant had finally intervened, insisting that the
little girl come back to Britain to be educated and live a
more settled life, and Cory's childhood had then been di-
vided between her grandparents' large house in Chelsea and
their Suffolk home, which she'd much preferred.

Sonia had eventually remarried, her second husband being American industrialist Morton Traske, and after his
death from a heart attack she'd taken up permanent resi-
dence in Florida.

Cory had an open invitation to join her, but her mother's
country-club lifestyle had never held any appeal for her.
And she suspected that Sonia, who was determinedly keep-
ing the years at bay, found her a secret embarrassment anyway.

Their relationship was affectionate, but detached, and
Cory found herself regarding Sonia very much as a way-
ward older sister. Most of the mothering in her life had
been supplied by her grandmother.

Beth Grant had been a serenely beautiful woman, con-
fident in the love of her husband and family. The loss of
her son had clouded her hazel eyes and added lines of sad-
ness to the corners of her mouth, but she had given herself
whole-heartedly to the rearing of his small daughter, and
Cory had worshipped her.

However, it hadn't taken long for Cory to realise there
was another shadow over her grandmother's happiness, or
to understand its nature.

The feud, she thought wearily. The damn feud. Still alive
even after all these years.

It had been the only time she'd known her grandparents
to quarrel. Seen tears of anger in Beth Grant's eyes and
heard her voice raised in protest.

'This can't go on,' she'd railed. 'It's monstrous—farcical. You're like children, scoring off each other. Except it's more dangerous than that. For God's sake, stop it—stop it now…'

Her grandfather's answering rumble had been fierce. 'He started it, Bethy, and you know it. So tell him to give it up. Tell him to stop trying to destroy me. To undermine my business—overthrow my companies.'

Arnold Grant had smiled grimly. 'Because it hasn't worked, and it never will. Because I won't allow it. Anything he does to me will be done back to him. And he'll be the one to call a truce in the end—not me.'

'The end?' his wife had echoed bitterly. 'What kind of truce can there be when you're trying to annihilate each other?'

She'd suddenly seen Cory, standing in the doorway, and had hustled her away, chiding gently.

'Gran,' Cory had asked that night, when Beth had come to tuck her into bed, 'who's Matt Sansom?'

'Someone who doesn't matter,' Beth had said firmly. 'Not to me, and, I hope, never to you. Now, go to sleep, and forget all about it.'

Wise counsel, Cory thought, grimacing, but sadly impossible to follow. And, since her grandmother's death six years before, the enmity between the two men seemed even more entrenched and relentless.

Only last week her grandfather had been gloating because he'd been able to filch a prime piece of real estate which Sansom Industries had been negotiating for from under their very noses.

'But you don't even want that site,' Cory had protested. 'What will you do with it?'

'Sell it back to the bastards,' Arnold had returned with a grim smile. 'Through some intermediary. And at a fat profit. And there isn't a damned thing that old devil can do about it. Because he needs it. He's already deeply committed to the project.'

'So he'll be looking for revenge?' Cory had asked drily.

Arnold had sat back in his chair. 'He can try,' he'd said with satisfaction. 'But I'll be waiting for him.'

And so it went on, Cory thought wearily. Move and counter-move. One dirty trick answered by another. And who could say what damage was being done to their respective multi-million empires while these two ruthless old men pursued their endless, pointless vendetta? It was a chilling thought, but maybe they wouldn't be content until one of them had been the death of the other.

And then there wouldn't be anyone to carry on this senseless feuding.

Cory herself had always steadfastly refused to get involved, and Matt Sansom's only heir was the unmarried daughter who kept house for him. There'd been a younger daughter, too, but she'd walked out over thirty years ago and completely disappeared. Rumour said that Matt Sansom had never allowed her name to be mentioned again, and in this case, Cory thought wryly, rumour was probably right.

Her grandfather's enemy was a powerful hater.

She shivered suddenly, and got up from her chair.

In her bedroom, she tossed her robe on to a chair and unhooked her bra. And paused as she glimpsed herself in the mirror, half naked in the shadows of the lamplit room.

She thought with amazement, But that's what he was doing—the man on the balcony—undressing me with his eyes. Looking at me as if I was bare...

And felt, with shock, her nipples harden, and her body clench in a swift excitement that she could neither control nor pardon...

For a moment she stood motionless, then with a little cry she snatched up her white cotton nightdress and dragged it over her head.

She said aloud, her voice firm and cool, 'He's a stranger, Cory. You'll never see him again. And, anyway, didn't you learn your lesson with Rob—you pathetic, gullible idiot? Now, go to bed and sleep.'

But that was easier said than done. Because when she closed her eyes, the dark stranger was there waiting for her, pursuing her through one brief disturbing dream to the next.

And when she woke in the early dawn there were tears on her face.

CHAPTER TWO

ROME walked into his suite and slammed the door behind him.

For a moment he leaned back against its solid panels, eyes closed, while he silently called himself every bad name he knew in English, before switching to Italian and starting again.

But the word that cropped up most often was 'fool'.

The whisky he'd ordered earlier had been sent up, he noted with grim pleasure. He crossed to the side table, pouring a generous measure into a cut-glass tumbler and adding a splash of spring water.

He opened the big sliding doors and moved out on to the narrow terrace, staring with unseeing eyes over the city as he swallowed some of the excellent single malt in his glass. He put up a hand to his throat, impatiently tugging his black tie loose, ignoring the dank autumnal chill in the air.

He said quietly, almost conversationally, 'I should never have come here.'

But then what choice did he have, when the Italian banks, once so helpful, had shrugged regretful shoulders and declined to loan him the money he needed to revitalise his vines and restore the crumbling house that overlooked them?

And for that, he thought bitterly, he had Graziella to thank. She'd sworn she'd make him sorry, and she'd succeeded beyond her wildest dreams.

He'd intended his trip to London to be a flying visit, and

totally private. He'd planned to stay just long enough to negotiate the loan he needed, then leave immediately, without advertising his presence.

But he'd underestimated his grandfather, and the effectiveness of his information network, he realised, his mouth twisting wryly.

He'd barely checked in to his hotel before the summons had come. And couched in terms he hadn't been able to refuse.

But he couldn't say he hadn't been warned. His mother had been quite explicit.

'Sooner or later he'll want to meet you, and you should go to him because you're his only grandchild. But don't accept any favours from him, *caro*, because there's always a payback. Always.'

Yet he still hadn't seen the trap that had been baited for him.

He'd been caught off guard, of course. Because Matthew Sansom had come to him first. Had simply appeared one day at Montedoro right out of the blue.

Rome had been shaken to find himself staring at an older version of himself. The mane of hair was white, and the blue eyes were faded, but the likeness was undeniable, and not lost on Matt Sansom either.

The shaggy brows had drawn together in a swift glare of disbelief, then he'd recovered. 'So—you're Sarah's bastard.'

Rome inclined his head. 'And you're the man who tried to stop me being born,' he countered.

There was a smouldering silence, then a short bark of laughter. 'Yes,' said Matt Sansom. 'But perhaps that was a mistake.'

He swung round and looked down over the terraces of vines. 'So this is where my daughter spent her last years.'

He sounded angry, almost contemptuous, but there was a note of something like regret there, too.

He stayed two nights at Montedoro, touring the *vigneto* and asking shrewd questions about its operation, and paying a visit to the local churchyard where Sarah was buried beside her husband, Steve d'Angelo.

'You have his name,' Matt said abruptly as they drove back to the villa. 'Was he your father?'

'No, he adopted me.'

The pale eyes glittered at Rome. 'Card-sharp, wasn't he?'

'He was a professional gambler.' Rome was becoming accustomed to his grandfather's abrasive style of questioning. 'He was also a brilliant, instinctive card player, who competed for high stakes and usually won.'

'And you followed in his footsteps for a while?'

Rome shrugged. 'I'd watched him since I was a boy. He taught me a lot. But my heart was never in it, as his was.'

'But you won?'

'Yes.'

Matt peered through the window of the limousine with a critical air. 'Your stepfather didn't invest much of his own winnings in the family estate.'

'It came to Steve on the death of his cousin. He'd never expected to inherit, and it was already run down.'

'And now you've taken it on.' That bark of laughter again. 'Maybe you're more of a gambler than you think, boy.' He paused. 'Did your mother ever speak about your real father?'

'No,' Rome said levelly. 'Never. I got the impression it wasn't important to her.'

'Not important?' The growl was like distant thunder. 'She brings disgrace on herself and her family, and it doesn't matter?'

Just for a moment Rome caught a glimpse of the harsh, unforgiving tyrant his mother had run away from.

'She was young,' he said, his own voice steely. 'She made a mistake. She didn't have to do penance for the rest of her life.'

Matt grunted, and relapsed into a brooding silence.

That was the only real conversation they'd had on personal subjects, Rome recalled. They'd seemed to tacitly agree there were too many no-go areas.

His grandfather had sampled the wine from Rome's first few vintages with the appreciation of a connoisseur, drawing him out on the subject, getting him to talk about his plans for the *vigneto*, his need to buy new vats for the *cantina* and replace the elderly oaken casks with stainless steel.

Looking back, Rome could see how much he'd given away, in his own enthusiasm. Understood how Matt Sansom had deliberately relaxed the tension between them, revealing an interested, even sympathetic side to his nature.

The offer of a low-cost loan to finance these improvements had been made almost casually. And the fact that it wasn't a gift—that it was a serious deal, one businessman to another, with a realistic repayment programme—had lured Rome into the trap.

It had only been later, after the deal had been agreed and his grandfather had departed, that he'd begun to have doubts.

But it was finance he needed, and repayments he could afford, he'd thought. And it would be a definite one-off. Once the last instalment had been paid, he would look for future loans from more conventional sources.

He remembered a night in Paris when both Steve and himself had emerged heavy winners from a private poker game which had been scheduled to last a week. The other players had been quietly spoken and beautifully dressed, and the air of power round the table had been almost tangible, and definitely menacing.

'Are we going back?' he'd asked eagerly, but Steve had shaken his head.

'Never return to a pool where tigers come to drink,' he'd told him, and they'd caught the next plane back to Italy.

It was a piece of advice that had lingered. But Rome had told himself that his grandfather's loan was a justifiable risk. The first and last visit to the tigers' pool.

Over the past two years communication between them had been brief, and usually by letter.

Rome had assumed that it would remain that way.

So the curt demand for his presence had been an unwelcome surprise.

Matt Sansom lived just outside London, in a house hidden behind a high stone wall and masked by clustering trees.

'Disney meets Frankenstein' had been Sarah d'Angelo's description of her childhood home, and, recovering from his first glimpse of the greystone, creeper-hung mansion, its bulk increased by the crenellated turrets at each end, Rome had found the description apt.

A quiet grey-haired woman in an anonymous navy dress had answered the door to him.

'Rome,' she said, a warm, sweet smile lighting her tired eyes. 'Sarah's son. How wonderful. I didn't believe we'd ever meet.' She reached up and kissed his cheek. 'I'm your aunt Kit.'

Rome returned her embrace, guiltily aware he'd assume she was the housekeeper.

He said, 'I didn't believe I'd ever be invited here either. I thought my existence was too much of a blot on the family honour.'

He was waiting for her to tell him that his grandfather's bark was worse than his bite, but the expected reassurance didn't come.

Instead, she said, 'He's waiting for you. I'll take you up to him.

'He's resting,' she added over her shoulder, as she led the way up the wide Turkey-carpeted staircase and turned left on to a galleried landing. 'He's been unwell. I was afraid it was his heart, but the doctor's diagnosed stress.'

If the house looked like a film set, then Matt Sansom's bedroom emphasised the impression. It was stiflingly hot and airless. The carpet was crimson, and so were the drapes, while the vast bed was built on a raised dais. And in the centre of it, propped up by pillows, was Matt himself.

Like some damned levee at eighteenth-century Versailles, Rome thought, amused, then met the full force of his grandfather's glare and realised this was no laughing matter.

He said, 'Good evening, Grandfather. I hope you're feeling better.'

Matt grunted and looked past him. 'Go downstairs, Kit,' he directed abruptly. 'You're not needed here.'

Rome swung around. 'Aunt Kit,' he said pleasantly, 'I hope you can make time for a talk before I leave.'

She nodded, darting an apprehensive glance at her father, then slipped from the room.

'You can bring us some coffee in half an hour,' Matt called after her as she closed the door.

Rome's brows lifted. 'Is that my aunt's job?'

'It is tonight. I've given the staff the evening off.' Matt gave him a measuring look. 'And you're very quick to claim family relationships.'

'Are you saying we're not related?' Rome asked levelly.

'No. I've decided to acknowledge your existence. But in my own time, and in my own way.'

'Am I supposed to be grateful?'

'No,' said Matt. 'You're expected to do as you're told.' He gestured at the carafe and glass on his night table. 'Pour me some water, boy.'

'As we're dispensing with common courtesy, may I tell you to go to hell, before I walk out?' Rome, tight-lipped, filled the glass and handed it to the old man.

'No,' Matt said. 'Because you can't afford to.' He allowed Rome to assimilate that, then nodded. 'Now, pull up that chair and listen to what I have to say.' He drank some water, pulling a peevish face. 'What do you know of Arnold Grant?'

Rome paused. 'I know that you've been lifelong business rivals and personal enemies,' he said quietly. 'My mother said that the feuding between you had poisoned life in this house for years. That's one of the reasons she—left.'

'Then she was a fool. She should have stayed—helped me fight him instead of disgracing herself.' He reached under his pillows and pulled out a folder. He extracted a magazine clipping and thrust it at Rome. 'Here he is.'

Rome gave the photograph an expressionless look. He saw a tall thin man with iron-grey hair, flanked by two prominent politicians.

He said, 'What of it?'

'I'll tell you precisely what.' Matt thumped the bed with his fist. 'He came at me again recently. I was negotiating for some land for a shopping development. I'd had plans drawn up, paid for test drilling and consultancy fees—and he did a secret deal—stole it from under my nose. Cost me hundreds of thousands of pounds, and not for the first time either. But, by God, it will be the last. Because I'm going for him, and this time it's personal.'

Rome was alarmed at the passion vibrating in the older man's voice. At the veins standing out on his forehead.

He said quietly, 'Someone once said the best revenge was to live well. Have you thought of that?'

'I intend to live well.' Matt's eyes glittered. 'After I've dealt Arnold Grant a blow he'll never recover from. And this is where you come in.' He paused. 'He has two weak spots—and one of them's in that photo. See the girl standing on the end?'

Rome gave the cutting a frowning glance. 'Yes.'

'That's his only granddaughter. She's not much in the way of looks but he thinks the sun shines out of her, and it's through her that I'm going to bring him down.' He paused. 'With your help.'

Rome put the cutting down, and rose. He said, grimly, 'Let's hold it right there. I don't know what you're contemplating, and I don't want to.'

'Always supposing you have a choice.' Matt leaned back against his pillows. 'Now, stay where you are and listen. You're going to meet this girl, and you're going to persuade her to marry you. I don't care how.'

For a moment Rome stared at him, then he said quietly and coldly, 'I'm not sure if this is a serious proposition, or a sick joke. If it's the first, the answer's no, and if the second, I'm not even marginally amused.'

'Oh, I mean it,' Matt said. 'And you'll do it. If you know what's good for you. Now sit down.'

The threat was unequivocal, and Rome felt tension grating across every nerve.

He thought, This is crazy. I have to reason with him...

Resuming his seat, he looked back steadily at his grandfather. 'I make wine. I don't take part in feuds. And I'm not interested in involvement with some unknown girl. There are plenty of tame studs for hire out there who'll fulfil your requirements. They might even enjoy it. I wouldn't.'

'You make wine,' Matt Sansom said softly, 'only while you still have a vineyard. If I called in my loan, you'd have to sell up. And believe that I'll do exactly what I need to.'

'But you can't.' Rome stared at him, horrified. 'I've made every payment...'

'But I'm having a cash-flow problem—I've just lost out on a big deal and have to recoup my losses.' Matt allowed himself a thin smile of satisfaction. 'And think of the consequences,' he added. 'Your workers will be out of jobs, your house will crumble into ruins, and you'll be picking a living from the casinos again. Is that what you want?'

Rome said, between his teeth, 'No.'

'Then be sensible. You'll have no problem with the Grant girl. There's no regular man in her life. She'll fall into your hand like a ripe apple from a tree.' He laughed hoarsely. 'She was engaged at one point, but threw her unfortunate fiancé, over a fortnight before the wedding. Nearly broke him up, I gather. You'll understand that, I dare say,' he added, darting Rome a lightning glance.

Rome was suddenly rigid. He said icily, 'You have done your homework.'

'Knowledge is power. And Arnie Grant doesn't know I have a grandson—which is his second weakness.'

Rome shook his head in disbelief. He said, 'You actually expect me to marry this girl—whatever her name is?'

'She's called Cory,' Matt said. Something flickered in his eyes, then vanished. 'It's a family name. But she's known as the Ice Maiden, because she freezes men off. And you won't marry her,' he added with a wheezing laugh. 'Because when Arnie Grant discovers your real identity— that you're my grandson and illegitimate at that—he'll move heaven and earth to stop it. To get rid of you from her life.

'That's why a hired stud won't do. It has to be you. Because Arnie Grant will want you to go away—to disappear before the truth comes out and turns him into a laughing stock, together with his precious child. And he'll pay you to do just that.

'But he'll know that I know,' he added gloatingly. 'That I set him up—and he'll have to live with that humiliation for the rest of his life. It will finish him.'

He nodded. 'You'll be able to name your own price, and whatever he offers you, I'll match. And you can consider the loan paid off, too.'

'I could do that anyway,' Rome flashed. 'I came over here looking for finance. I can repay you from my new borrowing. I don't need your dirty bargain.'

'Ah,' Matt said softly. 'But you may find that money's not as readily available to you as you thought. That you're not considered a good risk. In fact, I'd offer generous odds that your luck—and your credit—have run out.'

Rome rose and walked out to the window. Afternoon was fading into evening, and a breeze was stirring the rain-soaked shrubs in the garden below.

He thought of the thick autumn sunlight falling on Montedoro, the rich gleam of the earth and the pungent scents of the *cantina*, and felt a bleakness invade his very soul.

The vineyard had become his life. Its workers were his people. He was not prepared to let them go to the wall.

He said without looking around, 'So, you've poisoned the wells for me. Did you do the same in Italy?'

'I didn't have to. A man called Paolo Cresti did it for me. He thinks you're having an affair with his wife.'

Rome swung back to face him. 'That's a lie,' he said coldly. 'I haven't set eyes on her since her marriage.'

Matt's smile was thin. 'That's not what she's let her husband believe. You should have remembered the old saying—hell have no fury like a woman scorned.'

Rome stared at him bitterly. 'I should have remembered much more than that,' he said. He walked back to the bed and picked up the cutting. 'Has it occurred to you that this girl may not find me attractive?'

'Plenty of women have, by all accounts. Why should she be an exception?'

'And I may not fancy her,' Rome reminded him levelly.

'But you'll fancy the money you'll get from old Grant.' Matt leered at him. 'Just keep thinking of that. And keep your eyes shut, if you have to.'

Rome's mouth twisted in disgust. He looked down at the photograph. 'This tells me nothing. I need to see her properly before I decide.'

'I can't argue with that.' Matt handed him an elaborately embossed card from the folder. 'A ticket in your name for a charity ball at the Park Royal Hotel tomorrow night. She'll be there. He won't. You can look her over at your leisure.'

There was a tap at the bedroom door, and Kit Sansom appeared with a tray of coffee.

'We shan't need that,' her father said. 'Because Rome is leaving. He's got some serious thinking to do.' His smile was almost malicious. 'Haven't you—boy?'

Rome hadn't spent all the intervening time thinking, however. He'd attempted to make contact with some of the financial contacts on his list, but without success, no one wanted to know him, he realised bitterly. Matt Sansom had done his work well.

And now, for Montedoro's sake, he was committed to

the next phase of this war of attrition between two mega-
lomaniac old men.

He groaned, and tossed down the rest of his whisky. If
ever he'd needed to get roaring, blazing drunk, it was tonight.

As he walked back inside to refill his glass, someone
knocked at the door of his suite. A porter faced him.

'Package for you, sir. Brought round by special messen-
ger.' He accepted Rome's tip, and vanished.

Frowning, Rome slit open the bulky envelope. He realised immediately that he was looking at a complete dossier
on Cory Grant—where she lived, how she spent her spare
time, where she shopped, her favourite restaurants. Even
the scent she used.

No detail too trivial to be excluded, he acknowledged
sardonically.

But it was chillingly thorough. Matt must have been
planning this for a long time, he thought. And the screwed-
up land deal was just an excuse.

He poured himself another whisky, stretched out on the
bed and began to read.

'You made me look a complete idiot,' said Philip. 'Walking
out like that.'

Indignation added a squeak to his voice, Cory thought
dispassionately. And who needed a man who squeaked?

She kept her tone matter-of-fact. 'I didn't think you'd
notice I was gone.'

'Oh, come off it, Cory. I told you—I ran into some old
friends—lost track of time rather. And I'm sorry if you felt
neglected.' He paused. 'But I'll make it up to you.' His
voice became chummy, almost intimate. 'Why don't we
have dinner? I promise I'll give you my undivided attention.'

Cory gave her cordless phone receiver a look of blank disbelief.

She said politely, 'I don't think so, thanks. We don't have enough in common.' Except, she thought, that your father is one of Gramps's main sub-contractors, and you realise you may have rocked the boat.

'Look, Cory.' He sounded hectoring again. 'I've apologised. I don't know what else you want me to say.'

'Goodbye would do quite well.'

'Oh, very amusing. Know something, Cory? It's time you got off that high horse of yours and came down to earth, or you're going to end up a sad old maid. Because I don't know what you want from a man. And I suspect you don't know either.'

She said, 'It's quite simple, Philip. I want kindness. And you just don't qualify.'

She replaced her receiver, cutting off his spluttering reply.

She should have let her answering machine take the call, she thought. She simply wasn't up to dealing with Philip's efforts at self-justification after her disturbed night.

And she wasn't up to dealing with the reasons for the disturbed night either.

With a sigh, she went into her tiny kitchen, poured orange juice, set coffee to percolate and slotted bread into the toaster.

Gramps would be next, she thought, eager to know how the evening had gone, and she'd make up a kindly fib to satisfy him.

Only it wasn't her grandfather who rang almost at once, but Shelley.

'Cory—are you there? Pick the phone up. I have news.'

Cory hesitated, frowning slightly.

Her 'hello' was guarded, but Shelley didn't notice.

'I've found your mysterious stranger,' she reported happily. 'I did a quick check, and he bought one of the last tickets. His name's Rome d'Angelo. So, the ball's in your court now.'

'I don't see how.'

Shelley made an impatient noise. 'Come on, babe. You won't find many men with that name to the square acre. I'd start with directory enquiries.'

'Perhaps—if I wanted to find him,' Cory agreed, her lips twitching in spite of herself.

'I thought he'd made a big impression.'

'But not one I necessarily wish to repeat.' God, Cory thought, I sound positively Victorian. She hurried into speech again. 'Thanks for trying, Shelley, but I've made a major decision. If I get involved again, I want someone kind and caring, not sex on legs.'

'You could have both. Isn't this guy worth a second look?'

'I doubt if he was worth the first one,' Cory said drily. 'I'm sorry, love. I'm a hopeless case.'

'No,' Shelley said. 'You just think you are. So, if you're not going man-hunting, what do you plan for your day?'

'I'm doing the domestic thing.' Cory narrowed her eyes to stare at a ray of watery sun filtering through the window. 'And I may go over to the health club for a swim later.'

'Well, take care,' Shelley advised caustically. 'Too much excitement can be bad for you. I'll call you next week.' And she rang off.

As Cory replaced her own handset, it occurred to her that the unknown Rome d'Angelo was almost certainly that kind of excitement. Bad for you.

And best forgotten, she told herself dismissively.

*   *   *

The health club was rarely very busy on Saturday mornings, and today was no exception. Cory found she had the pool virtually to herself. She had always loved swimming, finding her own grace and co-ordination when she was in the water, and she could feel the tensions floating out of her as she cut through the water.

Afterwards she relaxed on one of the comfortable padded benches set back around the pool, and read some of the book she'd brought with her, but to her annoyance she found her concentration fragmenting.

In spite of herself, she kept thinking of the previous evening, and that brief, disturbing glimpse she'd had of Rome d'Angelo.

She found herself trying the name over in her mind, silently cursing Shelley as she did so.

I really didn't need to know his identity, she thought. He was easier to keep at bay when he was an anonymous stranger.

Although she'd been aware of a connection between them, as powerful as an electric current.

Suddenly, shockingly, she felt her body stir with excitement, as if she'd been touched. As if her mouth had been kissed, and her breast stroked gently to pleasure. Beneath the cling of her Lycra swimsuit her nipples were hardening to a piercing intensity, her body moistening in longing.

Cory sat up, pushing her hair back from her face.

It's time I took a shower, she thought, her mouth twisting. And maybe I should make it a cold one.

The changing rooms on the floor above were reached by lift. The women's section was beautifully equipped, with mounds of fluffy towels, gels and body lotions and other toiletries, hairdriers, and a selection of all the popular fragrances in tester bottles for the clients to try.

Cory didn't linger today as she usually did. She showered swiftly, then dressed in her usual weekend uniform of jeans and a plain white tee shirt.

She'd have some lunch at the salad bar on the ground floor before it got busy, she decided, as she shrugged on her leather jacket and picked up her tote bag. She was on her way out when she swung round, went back to the vanity unit, and sprayed her throat and wrists with some of her favourite 'Dune'.

And why not? she demanded silently as she made for the wide central stairway.

She was two thirds of the way down, head bent, moving fast, when she suddenly felt her warning antennae switch to full alert, and glanced up, startled.

She saw him at once, standing at the bottom of the stairs, looking up at her.

Recognition was instant, sending her pulses into overdrive.

She felt her lips frame his name, then stiffened in sudden, almost violent negation. Because he couldn't be here—he *couldn't be...*

Her foot caught the moulded edge of the step, and she stumbled. As she fell, she grabbed at the rail and managed to check her headlong descent, but she couldn't prevent herself sliding down the last half-dozen steps on her hip, and landing in an untidy huddle at his feet.

She lay for a moment, winded, hearing a buzz of comment, aware of shocked faces looking down at her. Of one face in particular, dark and coolly attractive, with vivid blue eyes fringed by long lashes, a high-bridged nose, and a mouth redeemed from harshness by the sensuous curve of its lower lip.

She realized too that he was kneeling beside her, and she was lying across his knees, his arm supporting her.

His voice was low and resonant with a faint accent she could not place.

'Don't try to move. Are you hurt?'

'No.' The denial was swift, almost fierce, and she pushed herself up into a sitting position. 'I'm fine—really. It was just a stupid accident.'

She was going to have the mother of all bruises on her hip, but she'd deal with that tomorrow. At the moment, her main concern was getting out of the club with what little remained of her dignity.

But his hand was on her shoulder, forcing her to stay where she was.

'Maybe I should take you to the nearest casualty room— get you checked over.'

'There's no need for that. No damage has been done.' She hunched away from him. She felt dazed, her body tingling, but instinct told her that had more to do with his hand on her shoulder than the tumble she'd just taken.

'Then perhaps you'd take me instead.' His face was dead-pan, but there was a glint in those amazing eyes. 'I'm not used to having girls fall at my feet, and shock can be dangerous.'

'Oh, really?' Cory glared at him as she hauled herself painfully upright. 'Now, I'd say you'd spent your adult life stepping over recumbent women.'

Oh, God, she thought, appalled. What am I doing? I can't believe I just said that.

His brows lifted. 'Appearances,' he said softly, 'can be deceptive. Something I also need to remember,' he added quietly as he, too, got to his feet.

Cory was almost glad to see one of the physiotherapists hurrying towards them. She answered his concerned questions, declined having her ankle examined, and agreed to fill out an accident report.

'But later.' Rome d'Angelo took her arm, and apparent control of the situation. 'Now the lady needs something to drink.'

Cory hung back, trying not to wince. She was altogether more shaken than she'd realised, but the fall was only partly responsible.

Now she needed to get away before she made an even bigger fool of herself.

She said, controlling the quiver in her voice, 'I'm really all right. There's no need for you to concern yourself any more.'

'But I am concerned,' he said softly, as the crowd began to melt away. 'You threw yourself, and I caught you. And I'm not prepared to put you down yet. So, are you going to walk to the coffee shop with me—or do I have to carry you?'

Cory heard herself say, 'I'll walk.' And hardly recognised her own voice.

CHAPTER THREE

THIS is lunacy, thought Cory, and I should run out of here and have myself committed immediately.

But she couldn't. For one thing, she was too sore to run anywhere. For another, her wallet and keys were in her tote bag, which Rome d'Angelo must have rescued after her fall and which was now hanging from one muscular shoulder as he waited at the counter in the coffee shop.

So, she said, perforce, to stay where she was, perched in rigid discomfort on one of the pretty wrought-iron chairs at the corner table he'd taken her to.

Round one to him, it seemed.

And all she had to do now was ensure there wasn't a round two.

Because every instinct she possessed was warning her yet again that this was a man to avoid. That he was danger in its rawest sense.

Anyone with a year-round tan and eyes like the Mediterranean was out of her league anyway, she reminded herself drily. But the peril that Rome d'Angelo represented went far deeper than mere physical attraction.

It's as if I know him, she thought restlessly. As if I've always known him...

She felt it in her blood. Sensed it buried deep in her bones. And it scared her.

I'll drink my coffee, thank him politely, and get the hell out of here, she thought. That's the best—the safest way to handle this.

She was by no means the only one aware of his presence,

41

she realised. From all over the room glances were being directed at him, and questions whispered. And all from women. She could almost feel the *frisson*.

But then, she certainly couldn't deny his eye-catching potential, she acknowledged unwillingly.

He was even taller than she'd originally thought, topping her by at least five inches. Lean hips and long legs were emphasised by close-fitting faded denims, and he wore a collarless white shirt, open at the throat. A charcoal jacket that looked like cashmere was slung over one shoulder, along with her tote bag.

He looked relaxed, casual—and powerfully in control.

And she, on the other hand, must be the only woman in the room with damp hair and not a trace of make-up. Which, as she hastily reminded herself, really couldn't matter less…

Pull yourself together, she castigated herself silently.

She saw him returning and moved uneasily, and unwisely, suppressing a yelp as she did so.

'Arnica,' he said, as he put the cups down on the table.

'Really?' Her brow lifted. 'I thought it was *café latte*.'

'It comes in tablet or cream form,' he went on, as if she hadn't spoken. 'It will bring out the bruising.'

'I think that's already escaped,' Cory admitted, wincing. She eyed him as he took his seat. 'You know a lot about herbal medicine?'

'No.' He smiled at her, his gaze drifting with deliberate sensuousness from her eyes, to her mouth, and down to her small breasts, untrammelled under the cling of the ancient tee shirt, and then back to meet her startled glance. 'My expertise lies in other areas.'

Cory, heart thumping erratically, hastily picked up her cup and sipped.

'Yuck.' She wrinkled her nose. 'This has sugar in it.'

'The recognised treatment for shock.' Rome nodded. 'A hot, sweet drink.'

'I fell down a couple of steps,' she said. 'I'm sore, but hardly shocked.'

'Ah,' he said softly. 'But you didn't see your face just before you fell.' He paused, allowing her a moment to digest that. 'How did you enjoy the ball?'

Pointless to pretend she hadn't noticed him, or didn't recognise him, Cory realised, smouldering.

She managed a casual shrug. 'Not very much. I didn't stay long.'

'What a coincidence,' he said softly. 'Clearly, we feel the same about such events.'

'Then why buy a ticket?'

'Because it was in such a good cause. I found it impossible to resist.' He drank some of his own coffee. 'Don't you like dancing?'

'I don't think it likes me,' she said ruefully. 'I have this tendency to stand on peoples' feet, and no natural rhythm.'

'I doubt that.' Rome leaned back in his chair, the blue eyes faintly mocking. 'I think you just haven't found the right partner.'

There was a brief, seething silence, and Cory's skin prickled as if someone's fingertips had brushed softly across her pulse-points.

She hurried into speech. 'Talking of coincidences, what are you doing here?'

'I came to look over the facilities.'

'You live in the area?' The question escaped before she could prevent it.

'I plan to.' He smiled at her. 'I hope that won't be a problem for you.'

Cory stiffened. 'Why should it?'

'My appearance seems to have a dire effect on you.'

'Nothing of the kind,' she returned with studied coolness. 'Don't read too much into a moment's clumsiness. I'm famous for it. And London's a big place,' she added. 'We're unlikely to meet again.'

'On the contrary,' he said softly. 'We're bound to have at least one more encounter. Don't you know that everything happens in threes?'

Cory said shortly, 'Well, I'm not superstitious.' And crossed her fingers under cover of the table. She hesitated. 'Are you planning to take out a membership here?'

'I haven't decided yet.' His blue gaze flickered over her again. 'Although, admittedly, it seems to have everything I want.'

'And separate days for men and women,' Cory commented pointedly, aware that her mouth had gone suddenly dry.

'Except for weekends, when families are encouraged to use the place.' His tone was silky.

Cory played with the spoon in her saucer. 'And is that what you plan to do? Bring your family?'

His brows lifted. 'One day, perhaps,' he drawled. 'When I have a family.' He paused again. 'I'm Rome d'Angelo, but perhaps you know that already,' he added casually.

Cory choked over a mouthful of coffee, and put her cup down with something of a slam.

'Isn't that rather an arrogant assumption?' she demanded with hauteur.

He grinned at her, unabashed. 'And isn't that a defence rather than a reply?'

'I don't know what you're talking about,' Cory said, feeling one of those hated blushes beginning to warm her face. Oh, no, she appealed silently. Please, no.

He said, 'Now it's your turn.'

'To do what?' *Fall over again, send the table crashing, spill my coffee everywhere?*

'To tell me your name.'

She said with sudden crispness, 'I'm grateful for your help, Mr d'Angelo, but that doesn't make us friends.'

'I'd settle for acquaintances?' he suggested.

'Not even that.' Cory shook her head with determination. 'Ships that pass in the night.'

'But we didn't pass. We collided.' He leaned forward suddenly, and, in spite of herself, Cory flinched. 'Tell me something,' he invited huskily. 'If I'd come down to the ballroom last night, and asked you to dance—what would you have said?'

She didn't look at him, but stared down at the table as, for a few seconds, her mind ran wild with speculation, dangerous fantasies jostling her like last night's dreams.

Then she forced a shrug, only to wish she hadn't as her bruises kicked back. 'How about, "Thank you—but I'm here with someone."?'

Rome's mouth twisted. 'He seemed to be doing a great job.'

'That's none of your business,' Cory fought back. 'Will you please accept, Mr d'Angelo, that I don't need a saviour, or a Prince Charming either.'

'And your circle of friends is complete, too.' He was smiling faintly, but those incredible eyes glinted with challenge. 'So what is left, I wonder? Which of your needs is not being catered for?'

Cory's face was burning again, but with anger rather than embarrassment. She said, 'My life is perfectly satisfactory, thank you.'

He was unperturbed by the snap in her voice. 'No room for improvement anywhere?'

'I have simple tastes.'

'Yet you wear Christian Dior,' he said. 'You're more complicated than you think.'

Suddenly breathless, Cory reached down for her tote bag, jerking it towards her. Then rose. 'Thanks for the coffee,' she said. 'And for the character analysis. I hope you don't do it for a living. Goodbye, Mr d'Angelo.'

He got to his feet, too. His smile held real charm. 'Until next time—Miss Grant.'

She'd almost reached the door when she realised what he'd said, and swung round, lips parting in a gasp of angry disbelief.

But Rome d'Angelo wasn't there. He must have used the exit that led straight to the street, she realised in frustration.

Her mouth tightened. So, he liked to play games. Well, she had no intention of joining in—or of rising to any more of his bait.

But at the same time she found herself wondering how he'd found out her name. And what else he might know about her.

And realised that the swift shiver curling down her spine was only half fear. And that the other half was excitement.

'You've met her? You've talked to her?' Matt Sansom's laugh rasped down the telephone line. 'You don't waste much time, boy.'

'I don't have a lot of time to waste,' Rome reminded him levelly. 'I have a life to get back to, and work to do.' He paused. 'But believe this. She isn't going to be any kind of push-over.'

'That's your problem,' his grandfather snapped. 'Failure doesn't enter the equation. What woman can resist being swept off her feet?'

In spite of himself, Rome felt his mouth curve into a reluctant grin as he remembered angry hazel eyes sparking defiance at him from the floor. Remembered, too, how slight she'd felt as he'd lifted her. Felt a small sensuous twist of need uncoil inside him as he recalled her pale skin, so clear and translucent that he'd imagined he could see the throb of the pulse in her throat as he'd held her. As he'd breathed the cool sophisticated fragrance that the heat of her body had released.

'This one could be the exception,' he drawled. 'But I've always preferred a challenge.'

'So when will you see her again?' Matt demanded eagerly.

Rome smiled thinly. 'I'll give her a couple of days. I need the time to find an apartment—establish a base.'

'I've told Capital Estates to prepare a list of suitable properties,' Matt barked. 'They're waiting for your call. And don't stint yourself. You need a background that says money.'

And he rang off.

Rome switched off his mobile and tossed it on to the bed, frowning slightly.

Well, he was committed now, and there was no turning back, he thought without pleasure. But Montedoro was all that mattered. All that could be allowed to matter.

And he had somehow to overcome his personal distaste for the means he was being forced to employ to save his vineyard.

Although, to his own surprise, not every aspect of the deal was proving as unpalatable as he'd expected.

Cory Grant was the last girl he would normally have pursued, but he could not deny she intrigued him. Or perhaps he just wasn't used to having his advances treated with such uncompromising hostility, he thought, his mouth twisting in self-derision.

Whatever, he'd enjoyed crossing swords with her in this preliminary skirmish.

The invisible circle still surrounded her, but within it she wasn't as prim and conventional as he'd thought. Under that ancient tee shirt she'd been bra-less, and at one moment he'd found himself, incredibly, fantasising about peeling the ugly thing off her, and discovering with his hands and mouth if her rounded breasts were as warm, and soft, and rose-tipped and scented as his imagination suggested.

But that wasn't in the equation either, he reminded himself grimly. Because he intended to keep all physical contact between them to an absolute minimum. He'd have quite enough to reproach himself for without adding a full-scale seduction to the total.

So, he was planning an old-fashioned wooing, with flowers, romantic dates, candlelit dinners, and a few—a very few—kisses.

Not as instantly effective as tricking her into bed, he thought cynically, but infinitely safer.

Because sex was the great deceiver. And great sex could enslave you—render you blind, deaf and ultimately stupid. Make you believe all kinds of impossible things.

Just as it had with Graziella.

He sighed harshly. Why hadn't he seen, before he'd got involved with her, that behind the beautiful face and sexy body she was pure bitch?

Because a man in lust thought with his groin, not his brain, was the obvious answer.

And at least he wasn't still fooling himself that he'd been in love with her.

In bed, she'd been amazing—inventive and insatiable—and he'd been her match, satisfying the demands she'd made with her teeth, her nails, and little purring, feral cries.

But when he'd asked her to marry him—laid his future and Montedoro at her feet—she'd burst out laughing.

'*Caro*—are you mad? You have no money, and the d'Angelo vineyard was finished years ago. Besides, I'm going to marry Paolo Cresti. I thought everyone knew that.'

'A man over twice your age?' He looked down at the lush nakedness she'd just yielded to him, inch by tantalising inch. 'You can't do it.'

'Now you're talking like a fool. Paolo is a successful banker, and wealthy in his own right.' She paused, avid hands seeking him, stroking him back to arousal. 'And my marriage to him makes no difference to us. I shall need you all the more, *caro*, to stop me from dying of boredom.'

For a long moment he looked at her—at the glittering eyes, and the hot, greedy mouth.

He said gently, 'I'm no one's piece on the side, Graziella.' And got up from the bed.

Even while he was dressing—when he was actually walking to the door—she still didn't believe that he was really leaving her. Couldn't comprehend his revulsion at the role she'd created for him.

'You cannot do this,' she screamed hysterically. 'I want you. I will not let you go.'

Up to her marriage, and for weeks afterwards, she'd bombarded him with phone calls and notes, demanding his return.

Then had come the threats. The final hissed vow that she would make him sorry.

Something she'd achieved beyond her wildest dreams, he acknowledged bitterly.

At first, he'd thrown himself into life at Montedoro with a kind of grim determination, driven by bitterness and anger.

But gradually, working amongst the vines had brought a kind of peace, and a sense of total involvement.

And that was something he wasn't prepared to lose through the machinations of a lying wife and a jealous husband.

Since Graziella he'd made sure that any sexual encounters he enjoyed were civilised, and strictly transient, conducted without recrimination on either side.

But Cory Grant did not come into that category at all, so it was far better not to speculate whether her skin would feel like cool silk against his, or what it would take to make her face warm with sensual pleasure rather than embarrassment or anger. In fact, he should banish all such thoughts from his mind immediately.

Even though, as he was disturbingly aware, he might not want to.

For a moment he seemed to breathe her—the appealing aroma of clean hair and her own personal woman's scent that the perfume she'd been wearing had merely enhanced.

He felt his whole body stir gently but potently at the memory.

Ice Maiden? he thought. No, I don't think so. And laughed softly.

'You're very quiet today.' Arnold Grant sent Cory a narrow-eyed look. 'In fact, you've been quiet the whole weekend. Not in love, are we?'

Cory's smile was composed. 'I can't speak for you, Gramps, but I'm certainly not.'

Arnold sighed. 'I thought it was too good to be true. I wish you'd hurry up, child. Help me fulfil my two remaining ambitions.'

Cory's brows lifted. 'And which two are those today?'

'Firstly, I want to give you away in church to a man who'll look after you when I'm no longer here.'

'Planning another world cruise?' Cory asked with interest.

Arnold frowned repressively. 'You know exactly what I mean.'

Cory sighed. 'All right—what's your second ambition?'

Arnold looked saintly. 'To see Sonia's face when she learns she's going to be a grandmother.'

Cory tutted reprovingly at him. 'How unkind. But she'll rise above it. She'll simply tell everyone she was a child bride.'

'Probably,' her grandfather agreed drily. He paused. 'So is there really no one on the horizon, my dear? I had great hopes you'd hit it off with Philip, you know.' He gave her a hopeful look. 'Are you seeing him again?'

Cory picked up the cheques she'd been writing for the monthly household bills and brought them over to him for signature. 'No, darling.'

'Ah, well,' he said, 'it wasn't obligatory.' A pause. 'What was wrong with him?'

This time she sighed inwardly. 'There was—no chemistry.'

'I see.' He was silent while he signed the cheques. As he handed them back, he said, 'Are you sure you know what you want—in a man?'

'I thought so, once.' She began to tuck the cheques into envelopes. 'These days, I'm more focused on what I *don't* want.'

'Which is?'

Eyes like a Mediterranean pirate, she thought, and a mouth that looks as if it knows far too much about women and the way they taste.

She shrugged. 'Oh, I've a list a mile long. And I need

to catch the post with these—and call at the supermarket before I go home. I haven't a scrap of food at home.'

'Then stay the night again.'

'Gramps—I've been here since Saturday.'

'Yes,' Arnold said. 'And I'm wondering why.'

'Does there have to be a reason?' Cory got up from the desk, the graceful flare of her simple navy wool dress swinging around her.

'Usually when you descend like this you have something you want to tell me.' His eyes were shrewd. 'Something on your mind that you need to discuss.' He paused. 'Or you're hiding.'

'Well, this time it was just for fun.' Cory dropped a kiss on his head on her way to the door. 'So, thank you for having me, and I'll see you tomorrow.'

She couldn't fool Gramps, she thought ruefully, as she posted her envelopes and hailed a taxi.

She'd gone straight home from the health club on Saturday, changed, thrown some things in a bag, and turned up on his doorstep like some medieval fugitive looking for sanctuary.

And all because Rome d'Angelo had known her name.

How paranoid can you get? She asked in self-denigration. It didn't follow that he also knew her address—or that he'd seek her out.

Although he'd said they would meet again, she reminded herself with disquiet. But perhaps he'd simply been winding her up because she'd made it so very clear she didn't want his company.

Undoubtedly he enjoyed being deliberately provocative, she thought, remembering the considering intensity of his gaze as it had swept over her, making her feel naked—as if all her secrets were known to him.

'A tried and tested technique if ever I saw one,' she

muttered to herself, and saw the cab driver give her a wary glance in his mirror.

For once, the supermarket wasn't too busy, and she had leisure to collect her thoughts, dismiss Rome d'Angelo from her mind, and concentrate on what she needed to buy.

She picked up some bread, milk, eggs and orange juice, then headed for the meat section. She'd buy some chops for dinner, or maybe a steak, she thought, sighing a little as she remembered the clear soup, sole Veronique, and French apple tart that Mrs Ferguson would be serving to her grandfather.

She swung round the corner into the aisle rather too abruptly, and ran her trolley into another one coming in the opposite direction.

She said, 'Oh, I'm so sorry,' then yelped as her startled gaze absorbed exactly who was standing in front of her.

'You,' she said unsteadily. 'What the hell are you doing here?'

'Buying food,' Rome said. 'But perhaps it's a trick question.'

'In this particular supermarket?' Her voice cracked in the middle. 'As in—yet another amazing coincidence?'

'I told you that things ran in threes.' He looked understated but stunning, in casual dark trousers and a black sweater, and his smiling gaze grazed her nerve-endings.

'So you did.' She took a breath. 'You're following me, aren't you? Well, I don't know what happens where you come from, but here we have laws about stalking—'

'Hey, calm down,' Rome interrupted. 'If I'm following you, how is it my trolley's nearly full, while yours is still almost empty? The evidence suggests I got here first.'

'Well, I'm damned sure you've never been in this shop before,' she said angrily.

'Because you'd remember?' He grinned at her. 'I'm flattered.'

'Not,' she said, 'my intention.'

'I believe you. And, actually, I'm here, like you, because it's convenient. I live just round the corner in Farrar Street.'

'Since when?'

He glanced at his watch. 'Since three hours ago.'

'You're telling me you've found a place and moved in— all since Saturday morning?' Cory shook her head. 'I don't believe it. It can't all happen as quickly as that.'

'Ah,' he said gently. 'That depends on how determined you are.' His gaze flickered over her, absorbing the well-cut lines of her plain navy coat, the matching low-heeled shoes, and her hair, caught up into a loose coil on top of her head and secured by a silver clasp. 'Another change of image,' he remarked. 'I've seen you dressed up at the ball, and dressed down at the club. Now you seem to be wearing camouflage.'

'Working gear,' she said curtly. 'Now, if you'll excuse me, I have my own trolley to fill.'

But he didn't move. 'You must take your job very seriously.'

'I do,' she said. 'I also enjoy it.'

'All appearances to the contrary,' he murmured. 'I thought British companies were adopting a more casual approach.'

'My boss is the old-fashioned type,' she said. 'And I must be going.'

Rome leaned on his trolley, his eyes intent as they examined her. 'I hoped it might be third time lucky,' he said softly.

'Tell me something,' she said. 'Does the word ''harassment'' mean anything to you?'

He looked amused. 'Not particularly. Now, you tell me

something. In these politically correct times, how does a man indicate to a woman that he finds her—desirable?'

'Perhaps,' Cory said, trying to control the sudden flurry of her breathing, 'perhaps he should wait for her to make the first move.'

Rome's grin was mocking. 'That's not an option I find very appealing. Life's too short—and I'm an impatient man.'

'In that case,' Cory said, having yet another go at tugging her trolley free, 'I won't keep you from your shopping any longer.'

Rome propped himself against the end of the shelving, and watched her unavailing struggles with detached interest.

'Maybe they're trying to tell us something,' he remarked after a while.

'Oh, this is ridiculous.' Cory sent him a fulminating glance, then shook the entangled trolleys almost wildly. 'Why don't you *do* something?'

His brows lifted. 'What would you like me to do?' he asked lazily. 'Throw a bucket of cold water over the pair of them?'

Cory's lips were parting to make some freezing remark that would crush him for ever when she found, to her astonishment, an uncontrollable giggle welling up inside her instead.

As she fought for control, Rome stepped forward and lifted his own trolley slightly, pulling the pair of them apart.

'There,' he said softly. 'You're free.' And he walked away.

Cory stood, watching him go.

So, that was that, she thought. At last he'd got the message. She knew she should feel relieved, but in fact her reaction was ambivalent.

She moved to the display cabinet, took down a pack containing a single fillet steak, and stared at it for a long moment.

Then, on a sudden impulse, she followed him to the end of the aisle. 'Mr d'Angelo?'

He turned, his brows lifting in cool surprise. 'Miss Grant?' The faint mockery in his tone acknowledged her formality.

She drew a breath. 'How do you know my name?'

'Someone told me,' he said. 'Just as someone told you mine—didn't they?'

Cory bit her lip. 'Yes,' she admitted unwillingly.

'So, now we both know.' He paused. 'Was there something else?'

'You were very kind to me when I fell the other day,' she said, stiffly. 'And I realise that my response may have seemed—ungracious.'

She paused, studying his expressionless face.

'I hope you're not waiting for a polite denial,' Rome drawled at last.

'Would there be any point?' Cory returned with a faint snap.

'None.' He sounded amused. 'Is that it—or are you prepared to make amends?'

'What do you mean?' Cory asked suspiciously.

Rome took the pack of solitary fillet steak out of her hand, and replaced it on a shelf.

He said quietly, 'Have dinner with me tonight.'

'I—couldn't.' Her heart was thudding.

'Why not?'

'Because I don't know you.' There was something like panic in her voice.

He shrugged. 'Everyone starts out as strangers. I'm

Rome, you're Cory. And that's where it begins. But the choice is yours, of course.'

She thought, And the risk...

In a voice she hardly recognised as hers, she said, 'Where?'

'Do you like Italian food?' And, when she nodded, 'Then, Alessandro's in Willard Street, at eight.'

Cory saw the smile that warmed his mouth, and her own lips curved in shy response.

She said huskily, 'All right.'

'Good,' he said. 'I'll look forward to it.' He turned to go, then swung back. 'And you won't need this.'

His hand touched her hair, unfastening the silver clasp, releasing the silky strands so that they fell round her face.

He said softly, 'That's better,' and went, leaving her staring after him in stunned disbelief.

CHAPTER FOUR

'YOU don't have to do this,' Cory told her reflection. 'You don't have to go.'

It was seven-fifteen, and she was sitting in her robe at her dressing table, putting on her make-up. And starting to panic.

She couldn't believe that she'd capitulated so easily—that she'd actually agreed to meet him, against all her instincts—and counter to her own strict code, too. Rule One stated that she never went out with anyone whose background and family were unknown to her.

And Rome d'Angelo could be anyone.

Except that he was quite definitely someone. Every hard, arrogant line of his lean body proclaimed it.

He walked away, she thought. And I should have let him go. It should have ended right there. And it certainly need not go any further.

She put down her mascara wand, and thought.

Rome d'Angelo might know her name, but that was all, she told herself with a touch of desperation. Her telephone number was ex-directory, and he couldn't know where she lived—could he?

On the other hand, these were obstacles that could easily be overcome by someone with enough determination.

So—she needed a contingency plan, she thought, frowning, as she fixed her favourite gold and amber hoops in her ears.

Well, she could always sub-let the flat and find somewhere else to live in a totally different part of London.

Somewhere she could lie low and wait for Rome d'Angelo to go back to wherever he'd come from.

As she realised what she was thinking, Cory sat back, gasping. Was she quite mad? she asked herself incredulously. Was she seriously contemplating uprooting herself—going into hiding to avoid nothing more than a casual encounter?

Because Rome d'Angelo wasn't here to stay. He was just passing through. She knew that as well as she knew the pale, strained face staring back at her from the mirror.

And he was clearly looking for amusement along the way.

But, on the scale of things, she would never be the number one choice for a man in search of that kind of diversion, she acknowledged with stony realism. So, why had he asked her?

Of course he was new in town, and probably didn't know many people as yet, but that would only be a temporary thing. A single man of his age with such spectacular looks would soon be snowed under with invitations. He wouldn't have enough evenings—or nights—to accommodate the offers that would come his way. Maybe she was just a stop-gap.

Cory grimaced as she fastened the pendant which matched the earrings round her throat.

For a moment she wished she was Shelley, who wouldn't hesitate to date Rome d'Angelo, whatever the terms, and who would frankly revel in the situation. And then wave him a blithe goodbye when it was over.

'You only live once,' Cory could hear her saying. 'So, go for it.'

And she wouldn't be able to credit the kind of heart-searching that Cory was putting herself through.

But then Shelley had never had someone like Rob in her

life, Cory reminded herself defensively. Had never known what it was like to suffer that level of betrayal. Never needed to armour herself against the chance of it happening again.

And yet, as Shelley had warned, Rob was in the past, and she couldn't use him as an excuse to shelter behind for ever.

She had her own private fantasy that some day in the future she'd meet someone kind, decent and reliable, who would love her with quiet devotion, and that she'd make a happy life with him. It was up there with the house in the country and the log fires, she thought with self-derision.

But, in the meantime, until that day arrived, maybe she needed to be more relaxed about men in general, so that she'd be ready for the man of her dreams when he showed up.

And Rome d'Angelo would be excellent material for her to practise on. To remind her, just for a short time, what it was like to talk, laugh and even flirt a little.

Because that was precisely as far as it was going. Flirting was fun—and it was relatively safe, too, because it was conducted at a distance.

She gave herself a long look in the mirror, noticing that there was a faint flush of colour in her cheeks now, and that her mouth glowed with the lustre she'd applied.

She'd brushed her hair until it shone, and it hung now in a soft cloud on her shoulders. As he'd stipulated, she thought, her mouth curling in self-mockery.

For a moment she recalled the swift brush of his hand as he removed the clip, and felt herself shiver with a kind of guilty pleasure.

As a gesture, it was pure cliché, of course, but still dev-astatingly effective. It had been several minutes before she'd been able to stop shaking, gather her scattered

thoughts, and finish her shopping in something like normality.

So, that was something she definitely could not afford,
she thought, biting her lip. To let him touch her again.

She got up and slipped off her robe. The simple flared
woolen skirt she put on was the colour of ivory, and she
topped it with a matching long-sleeved sweater in ribbed
silk.

She checked the contents of her bag, flung a fringed
chestnut-coloured wrap round her shoulders, and left.

It was only a five-minute walk to Alessandro's, and she
found her steps slowing as she approached, taking time out
to look in the windows of the boutiques and antiques shops
which lined the quiet street.

The last thing she wanted was to get there first, and let
him find her waiting. She might as well have 'needy' tat-
tooed across her forehead.

Of course, he might not be there at all, she realised,
halting a few yards from the restaurant's entrance. Perhaps
he'd instantly regretted his impulsive proposition and decided to stand her up instead.

Which would be neither kind nor considerate, but would
certainly solve a lot of problems.

She peered cautiously through the window, into the black
glass and marble of the foyer bar. It was already crowded,
yet she saw him at once.

He was leaning against the bar, and he wasn't alone. He
was smiling down into the upraised face of a dynamically
pretty redhead in a minimalistic black dress and the kind
of giddy high heels that Cory had never contemplated wearing in her life.

She was standing about as close to him as it was possible
to get without being welded there, and one predatory
scarlet-tipped hand was resting on his arm.

As Cory watched, her whole body rigid, the other girl reached into her bag and produced a card which she tucked into the top pocket of Rome's shirt.

Cory felt as if she'd been punched in the stomach. She wasn't prepared for the pain that slashed at her. Pain that came from anger, and something less easy to define or understand.

Her lips parted in a soundless gasp, and for a moment she was tempted to slip away into the night. Then some new arrivals came up behind her, and one of the men was holding the door for her, and smiling, and she was being swept along with the crowd into the restaurant.

Rome was looking towards the door, scanning the new arrivals, and when he saw Cory he straightened and, with a swift word to his companion, began to make his way over to her.

He was wearing light grey trousers which moulded his lean hips and emphasised his long legs, a charcoal shirt, open at the throat with the sleeves turned back over tanned forearms, and an elegant tweed jacket slung over one shoulder.

He moved with a kind of controlled power, and as the crowd parted to allow him through, heads turned to look at him.

Cory stood helplessly, staring at him, as the force of his attraction tightened her throat.

He said, '*Mia cara*, I thought you would never come.'

And before Cory could move or speak, she found herself pulled into his arms, and his mouth was possessing hers in a long, hard kiss.

She was too stunned to struggle, or protest. And if she had it would have made little difference. The arms holding her were too strong. The lips on hers too insistent. All she could do was stand there—and endure...

When he let her go at last, there were two angry spots of colour burning in her face. She was aware of amused stares, and murmured remarks around them.

She said in a fierce strangled whisper, 'How dare you?'

He looked amused. 'It took great courage, I admit, but, as you saw, it was an emergency.'

She said coldly, 'I imagine you can take care of yourself. You didn't need to drag me into it.'

'Perhaps,' he said. 'But the temptation was irresistible.'

'Then I hope you find having dinner alone equally appealing.' Her voice bit, and she half turned.

'No,' he said. 'I should not.' He made a brief, imperative gesture with one hand, and Cory suddenly found herself surrounded. A hostess appeared beside her to take her wrap, a waiter was asking deferentially what the *signorina* would like to drink, and Alessandro himself, wreathed in smiles, was waiting to conduct them to their table.

Somehow, walking out had become impossible. Unless she made the kind of scene which made her blood run cold.

Tight-lipped, she took her seat, and accepted the menu she was handed.

He said, 'Thank you for staying.'

Her voice was taut. 'You speak as if I had some choice in the matter.'

'Is that going to rankle all evening?' His brows lifted, and he spoke seriously. 'I've made you very angry, and I'm sorry, but it was a situation calling for drastic action. The lady was becoming persistent.'

'And you couldn't cope?' Cory lifted her eyebrows in exaggerated scepticism. 'You amaze me. And most men would be flattered,' she added.

'I'm not most men.'

'I've noticed,' Cory said with faint asperity. 'Yet you took her card.'

She stopped dead, aghast at another piece of blatant self-betrayal.

I should have been cool, she berated herself. Shrugged the whole thing off, instead of letting him know I'd noticed every detail. My stupid, stupid tongue...

'I was brought up to be polite,' Rome returned across her stricken silence. He removed the little pasteboard oblong from his pocket and tore it into small pieces, depositing the fragments in a convenient ashtray. 'But I prefer to do my own hunting,' he added softly, the blue eyes seeking hers across the table.

'I've noticed that, too,' Cory said. 'And you're also very persistent.'

He sent her a questioning glance. 'You have a problem with that?'

She shrugged. 'How you conduct your private life is no business of mine. You're an available man. You can please yourself whom you see.'

'Not always,' he said. 'Not when the lady remains evasive. Or even hostile.'

He was silent for a moment, then he said evenly, 'We haven't got off to a very good start, Cory. So, if I've ruined everything, and you really want to go, I won't stop you.'

She believed him. But the waiter was bringing their drinks, and a dish of mixed olives, and suddenly it all seemed too complicated. Besides, the performance so far had attracted quite enough attention, she reminded herself wryly.

He added, 'But I hope you won't.'

'Why should it matter?'

'As I've already indicated, I hate eating alone.'

Her voice was flat. 'Oh.'

'Among other reasons,' he went on casually. He paused.

'But perhaps I should keep those to myself, in case I put you to flight after all.'

His gaze captured hers, mesmerising her, then moved with cool deliberation to her mouth. She felt her skin warm under his scrutiny—her pulses leap, swiftly, disturbingly.

She managed to keep her voice under control. 'I suspect I'm actually too hungry to leave.'

His mouth curved into a faint grin. 'So it's worth enduring a couple of hours of my company for the sake of Alessandro's food?'

'I don't know,' Cory said composedly. 'They might have changed the chef.' And she picked up the menu and began to read it.

A small victory, she thought, as his brows lifted in amused acknowledgment, proving that she might be reeling, but she wasn't out.

When they'd given their order, Rome said, 'So—what arc the rules of engagement?'

She looked at him questioningly. 'What do you mean?'

'Kisses are clearly forbidden.' He gave a slight shrug. 'I was wondering whether there are any more taboos you're meaning to impose.'

'I already broke my major rule simply by turning up tonight,' she said. 'I think that's enough for one evening.'

'Ah,' he said softly. 'But this particular night is still very young.'

Cory took a sip of her Campari and soda. 'Perhaps we could dispense with comments like that.'

He shrugged a shoulder. 'Very well. Shall I say instead how mild it is for the time of year? Or calculate how many shopping days are left until Christmas?'

Cory bit her lip. 'Now you're being absurd.'

'And you, Miss Grant, are being altogether too serious.'

He studied her for a moment. 'Do you behave like this with all your dates?'

'I usually know them rather better than I know you.'

Remembering the squeaking Philip and other disasters, Cory surreptitiously crossed her fingers under cover of the tablecloth.

'Never a move without the safety net in place,' Rome mocked.

She lifted her chin. 'Perhaps. What's wrong with that?'

'Don't you ever get sick of security? Tired of measuring every step?' The blue eyes danced, challenging her. 'Aren't you ever tempted to live dangerously, Cory *mia*?'

She met his glance squarely. 'I thought that was what I was doing.' She leaned forward suddenly, clenched fists on the table. 'Why am I here tonight—having dinner with—a mysterious stranger?'

'Is that how you see me?' he was openly amused.

'Of course. You appear out of nowhere, and then you're suddenly all round me—in my face at every turn. I don't understand what's going on.'

'I saw you,' he said quietly. 'I wanted to know you better. Is that so surprising?'

Yes, she thought. *Yes.*

She lifted her chin. 'Why—because you felt sorry for me—leading contender in the Worst Dressed Woman contest?'

He said slowly, 'I promise you—pity never entered my mind.' There was an odd silence, then he went on, 'So— what can I do to become less of a mystery?'

'You could answer a few questions.'

He poured some mineral water for them both. 'Ask what you want.'

Cory hesitated, wondering where to begin. 'Why are you called Rome?'

'Because I was born there.' He shrugged. 'I guess my mother was short on inspiration at the time.'

'What about your father?'

Rome's mouth twisted. 'He wasn't around to ask. I never even knew his name.'

'Oh.' Cory digested that. 'I'm sorry.'

'There's no need,' he told her levelly. 'My mother made a mistake, but she had enough wisdom to know that it didn't have to become a life sentence. That she could survive on her own.'

'But it can't have been easy for her.'

'Life,' he said, 'is not a cushion.' He paused. 'Or not for most of us, anyway.'

Sudden indignation stiffened her. 'Is that aimed at me?'

'Are you saying you've grown up in hardship?' There was a strange harshness in his tone.

'Materially, no,' Cory said curtly. 'But that's not everything. And you're not exactly on the breadline yourself if you can afford a place in Farrar Street, over-priced tickets to charity bashes, and the joining fee at the health club.'

He shrugged. 'I make a living.'

'And how do you do that?' she said. 'Or is that part of your mystery?'

'Not at all.' Rome smiled at her, unfazed by the snip in her voice. 'I sell wine.'

'You're a wine merchant?' Cory was disconcerted. There was something about him, she thought, something rough-edged and vigorous that spoke of the open air, not vaults full of dusty bottles.

'Not exactly,' he said. 'Because the only wine on offer is my own.'

She stared at him. 'You own a vineyard?'

'Own it, work in it—and love it.'

His voice was soft, suddenly, almost caressing. This was

a man with a passion, Cory realised. And the first chink he'd shown in his armour.

Would his voice gentle in the same way when he told a woman he loved her? she wondered. And had he ever said those words and meant them?

Instantly she stamped the questions back into her sub-conscious. These were not avenues she should be exploring.

She hurried back into speech. 'And is that why you're in London? To sell your wine?'

A selling trip was unlikely to last long, she thought, and soon he would be gone and her life could return to its cherished quiet again, without troubling thoughts or wild dreams.

'Partly,' he said. 'I'm always looking for new markets for my wine, of course, but this time I have other business to transact as well. So my stay will be indefinite,' he added silkily. 'If that's what you were wondering.'

Wine-grower and part-time mind-reader, Cory thought, biting her lip.

It was a relief when the waiter arrived to take their order, and there were decisions to be made about starting with pasta or a risotto, and whether she should have calves liver or chicken in wine to follow.

When everything, including the choice of wine, had been settled, and they were alone again, he said, 'Now may I ask you some personal questions?'

'I don't know.' She could feel herself blushing faintly as she avoided his gaze. 'Maybe we should keep the conver-sation general.'

'Difficult,' he said. 'Unless we sit at separate tables with our backs to each other. You see, *mia bella*, you're some-thing of a mystery yourself.'

She shook her head, attempting a casual laugh. 'My life's an open book.'

'If so, I find the opening chapters immensely intriguing,' Rome drawled. 'I keep asking myself who is the real Cory Grant?'

Her flush deepened. 'I—I don't understand.'

'Each time we meet I see a different woman,' he said softly. 'A new and contrasting image. The silver dress was too harsh for you, but tonight you're like some slender ivory flower brushed with rose. The effect is—breathtaking.'

Cory discovered she was suddenly breathless herself. She tried to laugh again. To sound insouciant. Not easy when she was shaking inside.

'Very flattering—but a total exaggeration, I'm afraid.'

'But then, you don't see with my eyes, *mia cara*.' He paused, allowing her to assimilate his words. 'So, I ask again, which is the real woman?'

Cory looked down at her glass. She said huskily, 'I can't answer that. Maybe you should just choose the image you like best.'

'Ah.' Rome's voice sank to a whisper. 'But so far that image is just my own private fantasy. Although I hope that one night it will become reality.'

His eyes met hers in a direct erotic challenge, leaving her in no doubt over his meaning. He wanted to see her naked.

She felt her pulses thud as she remembered her certainty that he'd been mentally undressing her at the ball, and her colour deepened hectically.

She said unsteadily, 'Please—don't say things like that.' And don't look at me like that, she added silently, as if you were already sliding my clothes off.

His brows lifted. 'You don't wish to be thought attractive—desirable?'

'Yes, one day—by the man I love.'

Oh, God, she thought. How smug that sounded. How insufferably prim. As if she'd turned into the heroine of some Victorian novel. And waited for him to laugh.

Instead he sat quietly, watching her, his expression unreadable.

At last, he spoke. 'Tell me, *cara*, why are you so afraid to be a woman?'

'I'm not,' she denied. 'That's—nonsense. And I really don't like this conversation.'

Rome's brows lifted sardonically. 'Have I broken another rule?'

'I'd say a whole book of them.' She wanted to drink from her glass, but knew that he'd see her hand trembling as she picked it up and draw the kind of conclusions that she could not risk.

'No kisses and no questions either.' Rome shook his head. 'You don't make it easy.'

She forced a taut smile. 'But life isn't a cushion. I'm sure someone said that once. And here comes our first course,' she added brightly.

She hadn't expected to be able to swallow a mouthful, but the creamy risotto flavoured with fresh herbs proved irresistible, and the crisp white wine that Rome had ordered complemented it perfectly.

She said, striving for normality, 'We should be drinking your own wine.'

'Perhaps next time. Alessandro and I are about to strike a deal. I came here early so I could talk to him.'

'Until you got sidetracked, of course.'

'Ah, yes,' Rome said meditatively. 'I wonder if she has a rule book.'

'If so, it'll be the slimmest volume in the western hemisphere,' Cory said acidly, and stopped, appalled. 'Oh, God, I sound like a complete bitch.'

'No.' Rome was grinning. 'Merely human at last, *mia cara.*' And he raised his glass in a teasing toast.

As the meal proceeded, Cory found to her surprise that she was beginning to relax, and even enjoy herself.

The conversation was mainly about food. It was a nice, safe topic, but even so Cory found herself silently speculating about the man opposite her, talking so entertainingly about Cajun cooking.

Rome's life might now be centred on an Italian vineyard, but it was obvious that he was a cosmopolitan who'd travelled extensively. There was still so much she couldn't fathom about him, she thought restlessly.

She wondered about his parentage, too. His mother presumably had been Italian, so he must have derived those astonishing blue eyes from his unknown father. An English tourist, she thought, with an inner grimace, enjoying a holiday fling with a local girl, then going on his way without knowing a child would result. However strong Rome's mother had been, she would have had to struggle in those early years.

And how had an illegitimate city boy ended up growing wine in the Tuscan countryside?

No, she thought. There were still too many unanswered questions for her to feel comfortable in his company. So it was as well she had no intention of seeing him again—wasn't it?

The tiny chicken simmered in wine and surrounded by baby vegetables was so tender it was almost falling off the bone, and Cory sighed with appreciation as she savoured the first bite.

'You are a pleasure to feed.' Rome passed her a sliver of calves liver to taste. 'You enjoy eating.'

'You sound surprised.'

'You're so slim, I'd half expected you to be on a permanent diet like so many women,' he acknowledged drily.

Cory shook her head. 'I'm not slim, I'm thin,' she said. 'But no matter how much I eat, I never seem to put on weight.'

He said softly, 'Perhaps, *mia cara*, all you need is to be happy.'

The words seemed to hang in the air between them.

She wanted to protest—to bang the table with her hand and tell him that she was happy already. That her life was full and complete.

But the words wouldn't come. Instead, she found herself remembering the scent of his skin, the hard muscularity of his chest as he'd held her. The warm seductive pressure of his mouth in that endless kiss...

And she felt the loneliness and fear that sometimes woke her in the night charge at her like an enemy, tightening her throat, filling her mouth with the taste of tears.

She bent her head, afraid that he would look into her eyes and see too much.

She said in a small, composed voice, 'Please save your concern. I'm fine. And this is the best chicken I've ever had.'

She resisted a temptation to refuse dessert and coffee and plead a migraine as an excuse to cut the evening short. Because something told her that Rome would recognise the lie, and realise he'd struck a nerve. And she didn't want that. Because already he saw too much.

Instead she embarked on a lively account of her one and only visit to Italy on a school cultural exchange visit.

'The school we stayed at in Florence was run by nuns,' she recalled. 'And every night we could hear them turning these massive keys in these huge locks, making sure we couldn't escape.' She lowered her voice sepulchrally, and Rome laughed.

'Would you have done so?' He poured some more wine into her glass.

'I got to a point where I felt if I saw one more statue or painting I'd burst,' Cory confessed. 'I never knew there could be so many churches, or museums and galleries. We never seemed to have a breathing space. And, really, I'd rather have spent every day at the Uffizi alone.'

'But you weren't allowed to?'

She shook her head. 'The teachers hustled us round the city at light speed. They seemed to think that if we stood still for a moment we might be abducted—or worse.'

'Perhaps they were right,' Rome murmured. He paused. 'Will you ever go back there?'

'Perhaps one day. To wander round the Uffizi at my own pace.'

He was silent for a moment. Then, 'Florence is a great city, but it isn't the whole of Tuscany,' he said quietly. 'There is so much else to see—to take to your heart.' He drank some wine. 'It would make a wonderful place for a honeymoon.'

Cory took a deep breath. 'I'm sure it would,' she said coolly. 'And if I should happen to marry, I'll keep it in mind.'

'You have no immediate wedding plans?' He was playing almost absently with the stem of his glass.

She said crisply, 'None—and no wish for any.'

'How sure you sound.' He was amused. 'Yet tomorrow you might meet the man of your dreams, and all your certainties could change.'

The last time I dreamed of a man, Cory thought with a pang, it was you...

Aloud, she said, 'I really don't think so.' She picked up

the dessert menu and gave it intense attention. 'I'll have the peach ice cream, please—and an espresso.'

'Would you like some *strega* with your coffee, or a *grappa*, perhaps?'

'Thank you,' she said. 'But no.' Because it's nearly the end of the evening, and I need to keep my wits about me, she added silently.

She ate her ice cream when it came, and sampled some of Rome's amaretto soufflé, too.

Alessandro himself brought the small cups of black coffee. He said something in Italian to Rome, who responded laughingly.

Cory was convinced they were talking about her. She was already planning in her mind how to couch her refusal when Rome asked to see her again, which she was sure he would.

Alessandro turned to her. 'You enjoyed your dinner, *signorina*?'

'It was wonderful,' she said. 'Absolutely delicious. Far better than the steak and salad I was planning.'

'So lovely a lady should never eat alone,' Alessandro told her with mock severity, and went off smiling.

To Rome, she said politely. 'Thank you. It was a very pleasant evening.'

'Pleasant?' His mouth was serious, but his eyes were dancing. 'Now, I'd have said—interesting.'

'Whatever.' Slightly disconcerted, Cory reached for her bag. 'And now I must be going. It's getting late.'

Rome glanced at his watch. 'Some people would say the evening was just beginning.'

'Well, I'm not one of them,' Cory said shortly. 'I have work tomorrow.'

He grinned at her. 'And anyway, you cannot wait to run away, can you, *mia cara*?'

He came round the table and picked up her wrap before she could reach it herself. As he put it round her, she felt his hands linger on her shoulders, and the faint pressure sent a shiver ghosting down her spine, which she told herself firmly was nerves, not pleasure.

She took a step away from him. Her voice sounded overbright, and her smile rather too determined as she turned to face him. 'Well—goodnight—and thanks again.'

His brows lifted mockingly. 'Isn't that a little premature?' he drawled. 'After all, I have still to see you home.'

'Oh, but there's no need for that,' she said quickly. 'It's only a short distance—'

'I know exactly where it is,' Rome interrupted. 'And I still have no intention of allowing you to return there unescorted, so let us have no more tiresome argument.'

She stared at him. Her voice shook a little. 'Is there anything—anything you don't know about me?'

He laughed softly, '*Mia bella*—I have only just begun, believe me. Now—shall we go?'

And she found herself walking beside him, out into the damp chill—and the total uncertainty—of the night.

CHAPTER FIVE

THEY walked in silence, not touching, but Cory was heart-stoppingly aware of the tall figure moving with lithe grace at her side. She had half expected him to take her arm or her hand, and was grateful for the respite. Which was all it was.

Because she had no idea what would happen when they reached their destination.

She couldn't feel shock or even mild surprise that, as she'd feared, he'd discovered where she lived. Not any more. Every defence she had seemed to be crumbling in turn.

Which one would be next? she wondered, with a slight shiver.

Rome noticed instantly, but misinterpreted her reaction.

'You're cold.' He slipped off his jacket and draped it over her shoulders.

'Thank you.' Her fingers curled into the warm, soft cloth, gathering it round her like a barricade. Which was a mistake, because inextricably mingled with the smell of expensive wool was the now familiar scent of Rome himself, clean, totally male and almost unbearably potent. Reminding her of those few pulsating moments in his arms when her shocked senses had not just breathed him—but tasted him...

She hurried into speech. 'But you'll be frozen.'

'I don't think so.' There was a smile in his voice. 'I spend too much out of doors in all kinds of weather.'

'Oh,' she said. 'Yes—of course.'

76

She could hear the click of her heels on the pavement, hurrying slightly to keep up with his long stride. The air was cool, and there was a sharp dankness in the air which made her nose tingle.

She told herself, with an inward sigh, 'It's going to rain.'

'Is that a problem for you?' His answer, laced with faint amusement, alerted her to the fact she'd spoken aloud.

'Not really.' A faint flush warmed her face. She didn't want him to think she was making conversation for the sake of it. 'If you live in England, you can't let rain bother you too much. And when we lived in the country everything— the grass, the leaves—was so washed and—fragrant afterwards, I even began to like it. But here in the city the rain just smells dirty.'

'You liked the country best?' His tone was reflective. 'Then what made you leave?'

'The house wasn't the same after my grandmother died,' Cory said, after a pause. 'Too many memories. So my grandfather decided to sell it and base himself entirely in London. I don't blame him at all for that, but I miss the old place just the same.'

'Where was the house?'

'In Suffolk.' Her voice was soft with sudden longing. 'There was an orchard, and a stream running through the garden, and when I was a child I thought it was Eden.'

'It was the other way round for me,' Rome said, after a pause. 'I was brought up in cities, and I have had to wait a long time to find my own particular paradise.'

'But you have it now?'

'Yes,' he said, with an odd harshness. 'I have it, and I mean to keep it.'

Cory turned her head to look at him in faint bewilderment, and stumbled on an uneven paving flag.

Instantly Rome's hand shot out and grasped her arm, steadying her.

She felt the clasp of his fingers echo through every bone, sinew and nerve-ending. Was aware of her body clenching involuntarily in the swift, painful excitement of response. Bit back the small gasp that tightened her throat.

Turned it into a breathless laugh instead. 'Oh, God—I'm so clumsy. I'm sorry. Perhaps it was the wine. I'm not accustomed to it…'

'You don't usually drink wine?' He looked down at her, brows lifting.

'Rarely more than one glass.' Her smile was rueful. 'So I'll never make your fortune for you. Isn't that a shocking admission?'

'It confirms what I suspected,' Rome said, after a pause. 'That you work hard, and take your pleasures in strict moderation.'

She wrinkled her nose. 'That makes me sound very dull.'

He smiled back at her. 'Not dull, *mia cara*.' His voice was suddenly gentle. 'Merely—unawakened.'

She stared at him, her lips parting in surprise and uncertainty. When he halted, it took her a moment to realise that they'd actually reached the front door of her flat.

And some kind of moment of truth, she thought, her heart lurching half in panic, half in unwilling excitement.

As she fumbled in her bag for her key, she heard herself say in a voice she barely recognised, 'Would you like to come in—for some more coffee?'

His hesitation was infinitesimal but fatal, cutting her to the core.

'I cannot *mia bella*.' He sounded genuinely regretful, but it was rejection just the same. 'I have to go back to the restaurant and close the deal with Alessandro.'

She said, 'Oh.' Then, 'Yes—I see.'

She rallied, fighting down the disappointment that was threatening to choke her. Fighting to conceal from him that he had the power to hurt her.

She said brightly, 'Well—thank you for a lovely meal.'

'The gratitude is all mine, Cory *mia*.' He took the hand she did not offer and raised it to his lips, turning it at the last moment so that his mouth brushed her inner wrist, where the telltale pulse leapt and fluttered uncontrollably at the brief contact.

'And perhaps I had better have my jacket,' he went on conversationally as he released her. 'Unless, of course, you wish to keep it.'

'No—no—here.' Almost frantically she rid herself of its sheltering folds and pushed it at him. 'Goodbye.' She turned away, stabbing her key into the lock.

He said softly, 'I prefer—goodnight.'

As the door opened at last, she allowed herself a quick glance over her shoulder, but he was already yards away, his long stride carrying him back to his own life—his own preoccupations.

Cory thought, So that's that, and went in, closing the door behind her.

Rome cursed savagely under his breath as he walked away. What in hell was the matter with him? he demanded silently. His grandfather had been right. She was ready to fall into his outstretched hands.

All he'd had to do was walk through that door with her and she'd have been his. Total victory with minimum difficulty, he thought cynically.

A victory that he'd wanted, starkly and unequivocally, as the unquenched heat in his body was reminding him. The whole evening had been building to that moment.

And yet—unbelievably—inconceivably—he'd held

back. Made a paltry excuse about an appointment that was actually scheduled for the next day.

And she'd known. The street lighting had taken all the colour from her face and turned her eyes into stricken pools.

And suddenly he'd found himself wanting to pick her up in his arms. To hold her close and bury his face in the fragrance of her hair, and keep her safe for ever.

Perhaps the wine had affected him, too, he derided himself.

Because he'd planned a verbal seduction only, he reminded himself tautly. He'd intended to entice her with spoken caresses and half-promises, and a hint of passion rigorously dammed back. Yet scrupulously ruling full physical possession out of the equation.

Probably because he'd never visualised it as a genuine temptation, he acknowledged ruefully.

So what had changed—and when?

At what moment had she ceased to be a target—and become a woman?

It was when I called her 'unawakened'—and realised it was true, he thought.

She'd been engaged to be married. It was unrealistic to suppose she hadn't been involved in a sexual relationship with her fiancé. Yet his experience told him that, sensually and emotionally, she was still a virgin.

That maybe the Ice Maiden image was born from disappointment rather than indifference. That all the potential for response was there, waiting, just below the surface.

He'd felt it all evening in the swift judder of her pulses when he'd touched her, in the tiny indrawn breaths she hadn't been able to conceal. And in the sudden trembling capitulation of her mouth as he'd kissed her.

Shock tactics, he'd told himself at the time, when he'd

seen her standing there, the wide eyes filling with accusation. An expedient designed merely to prevent her from sweeping out and reducing his chances of saving Montedoro to nil.

He hadn't expected to enjoy it so much. Or to want so much more so soon either. That was an added complication he could well do without.

That, indeed, he *would* do without. Because he wasn't some adolescent at the mercy of his hormones, he reminded himself bluntly. He had control, and he would use it from now on.

But he hadn't anticipated Cory Grant's own hunger, he thought, his mouth tightening.

He realised now what it must have cost her to issue that faltering invitation. Had seen the shock in her eyes when he'd stepped back.

But perhaps in the greater scheme of things that was no bad thing, he told himself tersely. He would stay away for a few days, he decided. Keep her guessing. Allow her to miss him a little, or even a lot, before he made another approach. And then, just when she thought it was safe to go back in the water...

Because he couldn't afford any softening, whatever the inducement. He had to stay focused—cold-blooded in his approach. He had too much at stake to allow any ill-advised chivalrous impulses to intervene.

And if he'd created an appetite in Cory Grant, he could use it. Feed it tiny morsels rather than a full banquet. Until she could think—could dream—nothing but him, and the denial he was inflicting on her senses.

And that voluptuous ache in his own groin would simply have to be endured for now, he thought grimly.

When all this business was behind him, and Montedoro was safe, he would indulge himself. Take a break in Bali or the Caribbean. Find some warm and willing girl looking for holiday pleasure, and tip them both over the edge during long hot moonlit nights.

Someone who did not have bones like a bird and skin like cool, clean silk. Or a wistful huskiness in her voice when she spoke of her childhood.

He sighed restlessly and angrily, and lengthened his stride.

The Ice Maiden, he decided broodingly, would have been altogether easier to cheat.

Cory leaned back against the door of her flat, staring sightlessly in front of her, trying to steady the jagged breathing tearing at her chest.

'I don't believe I did that.' Her voice was a hoarse, angry whisper. 'I can't believe I said that.'

I'm not drunk, she thought. Therefore I must be mad. Totally out of my tree.

And now, somehow, I have to become sane again. Before I end up in real trouble.

She shuddered, crossing her arms defensively across her breasts.

She'd just issued the most dangerous invitation in her life—and somehow she'd been let off the hook. Rome had turned her down, for reasons she couldn't even begin to fathom but for which she had to be grateful, she told herself resolutely.

Only, she didn't feel grateful. She felt bewildered, bruised and reeling. Lost, even. And humiliated in a way she'd sworn would never happen again.

She eased herself slowly away from the door and fastened the bolt and the security chain before heading for her bedroom. She didn't put on any of the lights. She just went in and fell across the bed, without removing her clothes or her make-up. Curling up in the dark like a small animal going to earth to escape a predator.

And a lucky escape it had been. For all the anguish of emotion assailing her, she could not deny that.

Because Rome and she inhabited two different worlds. And the fact that those worlds had briefly collided meant nothing. Because soon he would be gone. Back to his vineyard and his real life. A life that did not include her but which would encompass other women.

And she would remain here, and go on working for her grandfather, as if nothing had happened. So it was important—essential—that nothing did happen. Or nothing serious, anyway.

She couldn't afford any regrets when Rome had gone.

Although it might already be too late for that, she thought, turning on to her stomach and pressing her heated face into the pillow.

Since that night at the ball, she'd scarcely had a quiet moment. He'd invaded her space, filled her thoughts, and ruined her dreams.

In the aftermath of Rob, she hadn't allowed herself to think about men at all. It had been safer that way. But just lately she'd had a few enjoyable fantasies about meeting someone whom she could love, and make a life with, and who would love her in return.

But even this cosy daydream had been snatched away. And in its place was a much darker image. One that churned her stomach in scared excitement, and made her body tremble.

It wasn't love, she told herself. It was lust, and she was ashamed of it. She'd believed she wanted Rob, but that had been a pallid emotion compared with this raw, arching need that Rome had inspired.

He seemed etched on her mind—on her senses. He was

in this room with her now. In this darkness. On this bed. His hands and mouth were exploring her with hot, sensuous delight, and she stifled the tiny, avid moan that rose in her throat.

I don't want this, Cory thought desperately. I want to be the girl I was before. I might not have been very happy, but at least my mind and body belonged to myself alone.

She also had to live with the shame of knowing that this need was purely one-sided. Because Rome had been able to walk away without a backward glance.

Yet her main concern was her own behaviour.

She'd never made the running with men—not even with Rob. She'd allowed him to set the pace throughout their relationship.

She was too shy—too inhibited—to set up an agenda that included sex on demand, even with the man she planned to marry.

Until now, tonight, when she had suddenly stepped out of character.

And much good it did me, she thought bitterly.

Although going to bed with Rome would have been an even greater disaster, for all kinds of reasons.

When she saw him again—if she saw him again—she would be safely back in her own skin, she told herself, and playing by her own rules. She would take no more risks. Especially with someone like Rome d'Angelo.

She would be back in control.

And the loneliness of the thought brought tears, sharp and acrid, crowding into her throat.

'Old Sansom's playing a cool game over this land deal,' Arnold Grant remarked. 'I was sure there'd be an approach from some go-between by now. So what's the old devil up to? What's he got up his sleeve now?'

He waited for some response from his granddaughter, and when none was forthcoming swung his chair round to look at her, only to find her sitting staring out of the window, not for the first time that day.

'What's the matter with you, girl?' he demanded. 'Are you in a trance, or what?'

Cory started guiltily. 'I'm sorry, darling. I guess I'm a bit tired.' She forced a smile. 'I was out on the town last night.'

'Quite right, too.' Arnold surveyed her, narrow-eyed. 'Although one night shouldn't put those shadows under your eyes. You look as if you haven't slept for a week. No stamina, you young ones.' He paused. 'So—who were you out with? Do I know him?'

Cory sighed. 'Yes, Gramps, you do indeed know *her*.' She stressed the pronoun. 'Shelley and I went to the cinema, then had a meal in a Chinese restaurant. I really enjoyed it.'

Which was pitching it a bit high, she silently admitted. The film had been good, the food delicious and Shelley great company, but Cory had been on tenterhooks in case her friend brought Rome d'Angelo into the conversation again, which had rather taken the edge off the evening.

I'm being thoroughly paranoid, she thought.

Arnold snorted. 'Well, you don't look or sound as if you had a wonderful time. You've been quiet all week, girl. Not your usual self at all.'

'In other words, I'm boring, and you're going to replace me with a glamorous blonde,' Cory teased.

'God forbid,' Arnold said devoutly. 'And you're not boring, child. Just—different.' He gave her a sharp look. 'Is it man trouble?'

'No,' Cory said, her throat tightening. 'No, of course not.'

It wasn't really a lie, she defended silently. Because there was no man to cause trouble—not any more.

She hadn't heard from Rome, or set eyes on him, all through this endless week.

She'd filled her days with activity—work, food-shopping, cooking, cleaning the flat to a pristine shine.

But the nights had been a different matter. Sleep had proved elusive, and she'd spent hours staring into an all-pervading blackness, longing for oblivion.

She'd used her answering machine to screen her calls, but she could have saved herself the effort because none of them had been from him.

On the street, her senses felt stretched to snapping point as she scanned the passers-by, looking for him. As she glanced over her shoulder, expecting to find him there.

Only, he never had been.

So that particular episode was clearly over and done with almost before it had begun, she told herself determinedly. Rome had found someone else to pursue—metal more attractive. And, in the long term, that was the best—the safest thing.

It was the short term she was having trouble handling.

'Money, then?' Arnold persisted. 'Are those sharks of landlords giving you trouble? Do you want my lawyers to deal with them?'

'Absolutely not,' Cory protested. 'They're a very reputable property company.'

'Hmm.' Arnold was silent for a moment. Then, 'If you've got yourself into debt, child, you can tell me. I could always raise your salary.'

'Heavens, no.' Cory was aghast. 'I don't earn half what you pay me as it is.'

'I'll be the judge of that,' her grandfather said gruffly. 'So what's the problem?'

Cory shrugged. 'It's nothing serious,' she prevaricated. 'It's probably all the wet weather we've had. I may be one of these people who needs the sun. I'm just feeling in a bit of a rut—not too sure where my life is going. That's all.'

It was his turn to sigh, his face set in serious lines. 'Ah, child. You need to go to parties. Meet more people. If my Beth hadn't been taken, she'd have seen to it. Arranged a social life for you. Made sure you enjoyed yourself.' He shook his head. 'But I'm no good at that sort of thing. I've let you down.'

'Oh, Gramps.' Cory's tone was remorseful. 'That's not true. And I hate parties.'

'Nevertheless, you need a change of air—a change of scenery,' Arnold said with decision. 'I'm going down to Dorset this evening, to spend the weekend with the Harwoods. Why don't you come with me? They're always asking about you. And that nephew of theirs will be there, too, on leave from the Army,' he added blandly. 'You remember him, don't you?'

Yes, Cory remembered Peter Harwood. Good-looking in a florid way, and very knowledgeable about tank manoeuvres. Keen to share his expertise, too, for hours on end. Not an experience she was anxious to repeat.

She said gently, 'It's a kind thought, Gramps, but I don't think so. I—I have plans of my own.'

And now he would ask what they were, and she would be floundering, she thought, bracing herself mentally.

But, blessedly, the phone rang, diverting his attention, and the awkward moment passed.

As she was preparing to leave that evening, Arnold halted her with a hand on her arm. 'Sure you won't come to Dorset?'

'Absolutely,' she said firmly.

He nodded glumly. 'Any message for young Peter?'

Her swift smile was impish. 'Give my regards to his tank.'

But she would do something positive this weekend, she determined. She wasn't going to waste any more time phone-watching.

Rome had appeared in her life, and now he had gone again, and she should be feeling thankful, instead of this odd hollowness, as if the core of her being had been scooped out with a blunt knife.

But I'll get over it, she told herself resolutely. I did before. I can again.

And as a first step, she didn't go to the health club in the morning. Just in case Rome had decided to use it after all and she ran into him there—literally as well as figuratively, she thought, remembering their previous encounter with a grimace.

Instead she'd go to Knightsbridge and indulge in some serious window shopping. Maybe have lunch at Harvey Nicks, and spend the afternoon at the cinema, or a theatre matinée.

Or she might go to a travel agency and book herself some winter sunshine.

Except that she already knew what she was going to do. What she always did when she was at a loose end, or troubled. Although she had no real reason to feel like that, she reminded herself. Not any more. Because, with luck, that particular trouble was past and gone.

Nevertheless, she would go to the National Gallery and look at the Renaissance paintings. It might be a very public place, but it was her private sanctuary, too. Her comfort zone.

And that was what her life needed at this particular moment, she thought. Not shopping, or long-haul holidays, but tranquillity and beauty.

She would let those exquisite forms and colours work their magic on her, and then, when she was calm and in control, with her life drawn securely round her once more, she would plan the rest of her day.

She dressed swiftly in a simple grey skirt with a matching round-necked sweater in thin wool, tied a scarf patterned in grey, ivory and coral at her throat, and thrust her feet into loafers. Then she grabbed her raincoat and an umbrella and set off for Trafalgar Square.

The Gallery was having a busy morning. Cory threaded her way between the school parties and guided groups of tourists until she reached the section she wanted. Thankfully, it was quieter here, as most of the crowds seemed to have been siphoned off to some special exhibition, and she wandered slowly from room to room until she found the *Mystic Nativity* by Botticelli and a seat on a bench facing it.

It had always been her favourite, she thought, as she drank in the clear vibrant colours. She loved the contrast between the earthiness of the kings and shepherds, come to do honour to the kneeling Virgin and her Child, and the ethereal, almost terrifying beauty of the watching angels.

Usually just a few minutes in front of it melted away any stress she might be experiencing. But today it wasn't having the desired effect, and after a while she got up restlessly and walked on.

She paused to look at another Botticelli—the great canvas of *Venus and Mars*—staring for a long disturbing moment at the languid beauty in her white and gold dress, with a world of secret knowledge in her face, and the conquered, sated man next to her.

What would it be like, she wondered, to have that kind

of sexual power? To bewitch a man, and leave him drained, and at your mercy?

Love winning the ultimate victory over war, she thought as she turned away.

She would go and get some coffee, she decided, and then probably revert to Plan A and the shopping expedition to Knightsbridge.

She was on her way out when she saw the portrait. She'd noticed it before on previous visits—a young man in his shirtsleeves, his curling hair covered by a cap, turning his head to bestow a cool and level glance on his observers.

But this time she went over to take a much closer look. She stood motionless, her hands clenched in her pockets, staring at the tough, dynamic face, with the strong nose, the firm, deeply cleft chin and the high cheekbones, as if she was seeing it for the first time.

Aware of the slow, shocked beat of her heart. Because, she realised, if Rome d'Angelo had been alive in the six-teenth century, he could have modelled for this portrait by Andrea del Sarto.

Since their first meeting she'd had the nagging feeling that she'd seen him somewhere before, and had been trying to trace the elusive resemblance. And now, at last, she'd succeeded. He'd been here all the time. In her sanctuary. Waiting for her.

She shook her head, her lips twisting in a little smile.

She said softly, 'Your eyes are the wrong colour, that's all. They should be blue. Otherwise you could be him—five hundred years ago.'

And heard, from behind her, as she stood, rooted to the spot in horrified disbelief, Rome's voice saying with cool dryness, 'You really think so? You flatter me, *cara*.'

CHAPTER SIX

CORY looked down at the polished floorboards at her feet, praying they would open and swallow her.

The last time she'd felt such a complete idiot had been standing on her own doorstep as Rome walked away, she thought detachedly, feeling the first scalding wave of embarrassment wash over her. And, before that, when she'd taken that spectacular dive at his feet.

Now she'd let him catch her standing there talking to herself, for God's sake. Speaking her thoughts aloud, as she often did. And this was once too often.

She turned slowly, her face still flushed.

He was standing about a yard away, unsmiling, the brilliant eyes slightly narrowed, his damp hair curling on to his forehead. He was wearing narrow black trousers, with a matching rollneck sweater, and carrying a russet waterproof jacket over one arm.

Cory lifted her chin in challenge. 'There's a saying about eavesdroppers.'

Rome nodded. 'I know it. But your comments were hardly derogatory. And you would never have made them to my face.'

'What are you doing here?'

'Just like you—looking at Renaissance paintings.'

'So, you just happened to—turn up?' Her tone was incredulous.

Rome shrugged a shoulder. 'I can hardly visit the Uffizi,' he returned coolly. 'But it's true that I hoped I'd find you here,' he added.

She wished she could stop shaking inside. She said haughtily, 'I can't imagine why.'

Rome's brows lifted. 'No, *mia bella*? I think you do your imagination less than justice. Except where this portrait is concerned.' He looked past her, studying it reflectively. 'Is this really how you see me?'

Cory's flush deepened. 'You can't deny there is a resemblance,' she said defensively. 'And he's not named in the portrait. He could be one of your ancestors.'

Rome's mouth twisted. 'I doubt it, but it's a romantic thought.'

'From now on I'll try and keep them under control,' Cory told him with bite. 'Do enjoy your art appreciation.'

As she made to walk past him, he detained her with a hand on her arm.

'You're not leaving?'

It was her turn to shrug. 'I've seen what I came to see.'

'And so have I,' he said softly. 'Another intriguing co-incidence. So—now we have the rest of the day ahead of us.'

She said thickly, 'You take a hell of a lot for granted, Mr d'Angelo. And I have other plans.'

'Do they involve anyone else?'

'That's none of your business.'

'A simple no would be enough.' The blue eyes were dancing suddenly, and her mouth felt dry. His voice was suddenly coaxing. 'Take pity on me, Cory *mia*. Cancel your arrangements and spend the day with me instead.' His smile coaxed, too. Disturbingly. 'Help me play tourist.'

She bit her lip. 'I don't think that's a very good idea.'

'You haven't given it a chance,' he said. 'It might improve on acquaintance and—who knows?—so might I.'

In response, her own mouth curved reluctantly. 'Don't you ever take no for an answer?'

'That, *mia bella*, would depend on the question.' His voice was silky. 'But I promise you one thing, Cory Grant. When you say no to me and mean it, I'll listen.'

There was a brief heart-stopping pause, then he said abruptly, 'Now, will you come with me? Share today?'

He held out his hand steadily, imperatively, and almost before she knew what she was doing she allowed him to take her fingers—clasp them.

He nodded, acknowledging the silent bargain, then moved off, making for the main exit, sweeping her along with him so fast that Cory practically had to jog to keep up.

She said breathlessly, 'Just a minute—you haven't told me yet where we're going.'

'First—to the car park.'

'You've—bought a car?'

'No, I've leased one.'

'And then?'

He gave her a swift sideways glance. He was smiling, but there was an unmistakable challenge in the blue eyes.

He said softly, 'Why, to Suffolk, of course, *mia cara. Avanti.*'

She said, 'It is a joke, isn't it? You're not really serious?'

They were out of London now, and travelling towards Chelmsford, as Cory registered tautly.

'Am I going in the wrong direction?' Rome asked. 'I was aiming for Sudbury.'

'No,' she said. 'No—that's fine. But I still don't know why you're doing this.'

The car was dark, streamlined and expensive, and he handled it well on the unfamiliar roads—as she was grudgingly forced to admit.

'I'm tired of concrete,' he said. 'I thought you would be, too.'

'Yes—but you don't just—take off for Suffolk on the spur of the moment,' Cory said warmly. 'It's a long way.'

'And we have the rest of the day.' He flicked a glance at her, a half-smile playing round his mouth. 'Would you prefer to turn back? Visit another art gallery—or perhaps a museum?'

'No,' she said slowly. 'No—I don't want to do that.'

She wasn't sure it was possible to turn back either. Not now. Not ever. She felt as if she'd taken some wild, momentous leap in the dark.

She said, almost beseechingly, 'But it's all happened so fast…'

'I think it was the way you talked about it,' Rome said, after a pause. 'I could tell how much it had meant to you. And I was curious to see something that could put that note of yearning into your voice. It made the distance seem immaterial.'

'Oh.' Her throat tightened.

'And I would do the same for you,' he added casually. 'If you come to Italy, I'd show you all the places that were important to me.'

'Even your vineyard?'

He laughed. 'Maybe even that.'

'Well, I hope you won't be disappointed in Suffolk. It's quite a gentle landscape. There aren't any towering cliffs or sweeping hills. And the beaches are all dunes and shingle.'

Rome shrugged a shoulder. 'I'll chance it.'

Cory watched curiously as he negotiated a busy junction with effortless ease.

She said stiltedly, 'You're a very good driver.'

'I've been driving for a long time.' He slanted a glance at her. 'You don't have a car?'

She shook her head. 'It's never seemed worth it. Not in the city. For work and shopping I tend to use the Underground, or taxis.'

'Unfortunately we don't have those conveniences at Montedoro, so one's own transport is a necessity.'

She nodded. 'Have you visited East Anglia before?'

'No,' he said. 'I've only been in London. Why?'

'Because you seem to know the way so well. And without any prompting from me.'

There was another slight pause, then he shrugged again. 'We have road maps even in Tuscany. And I'm capable of working out a route for a journey.'

'Which means you must have planned this in advance,' Cory said slowly. She turned her head, staring at him. 'Yet you had no means of knowing that we'd meet today. Or ever again, for that matter.'

'You're wrong about that.' His voice was quiet. 'Because I knew I would see you again, Cory *mia*. And so did you. If not today, then at some other time. And I could wait.'

Yes, she thought, with a sudden pang. He would be good at that. Was that why he'd kept away all week? Making her wait—making her wonder?

She said bitterly, 'I don't think I know anything any more.'

'Do you wish you hadn't come? Perhaps you'd rather be back at your National Gallery, fantasising about an image on canvas.' His tone was sardonic. 'Do you prefer oil paint to flesh and blood, *mia*?'

She flushed. 'That's a hateful thing to say. And not true.'

'I'm relieved to hear it.'

Cory bit her lip. Glancing up at the sky, she said, with

asperity, 'It seems to have stopped raining. I suppose you arranged that, too.'

Rome laughed. 'Of course. I want this to be a perfect day for you, *cara*.'

Cory relapsed into a brooding silence. But it didn't last long—how could it, when she began to recognise familiar landmarks and favourite bits of countryside?

In spite of herself, she felt anticipation—even happiness—beginning to uncurl inside her.

'We'll be in Sudbury soon,' Rome remarked at last. 'Do you want to stop and look round?'

'Gainsborough was born there,' she said. 'They've turned the house into a gallery for some of his work. But maybe we've looked at enough paintings for one day.'

'Where do you suggest we go instead?'

'Lavenham's quite near,' she said. 'And it's really beautiful—full of old, timbered houses.'

'Is that where you used to live?'

She shook her head. 'No, our house was nearer the coast—in a village called Blundham.'

'I'd very much like to see it,' Rome said, after a pause. 'Would you mind?'

'No,' she said. 'Why should I? But, at the same time, why should you want to?'

'To fill in another piece of the puzzle.' He was smiling again, but his voice was serious. 'To know you better, *mia bella*.'

Cory straightened in her seat. She said crisply, 'Isn't that rather a waste of time—when you'll be gone so soon?'

He said softly, 'At the moment, my plans are fluid.' And paused. 'Tell me, is there somewhere in Lavenham that we can have lunch?'

She said huskily, 'Several places.' And stared determinedly out of the window as she allowed herself to wonder what he might mean.

The bar at the Swan Hotel opened into a maze of small rooms. They found a secluded alcove furnished with a large comfortable sofa and a small table, and a cheerful waitress brought them home-made vegetable soup followed by generous open sandwiches, with smoked salmon for Cory and rare roast beef for Rome. She chose a glass of white wine, dry with an underlying flowery taste, while Rome drank a sharp, icy Continental beer.

On their way to the hotel they'd visited the market place and seen the old Corpus Christi guildhall, now a community centre, and the ancient market cross.

The rain had well and truly stopped now, and a watery sun was making occasional appearances between the clouds, accompanied by a crisp breeze.

Cory was telling him over the sandwiches that a number of the shops they'd passed dated from the Tudor period, when she stopped with a rueful laugh.

'What am I doing?' She shook her head almost despairingly. 'I'm trying to teach history to someone who was born in Rome.'

He grinned. 'Different history, Cory *mia*. And don't stop, please. I'm enjoying my lesson. Why was Lavenham important?'

'Because of the wool trade. It was a major centre. Then came the Industrial Revolution, and the power looms, but there was no coal locally to run them, so the woollen industry moved north.' She smiled rather sadly. 'We may have missed out on the dark, satanic mills, but now we have nuclear power plants instead.'

'So, tell me about Blundham.'

'I'm afraid you'll be disappointed.' Cory finished her

wine. 'It's just an ordinary little village. We don't get too many tourists, apart from birdwatchers and walkers.'

'I hope our arrival won't prove too much of a shock,' Rome said drily, as he paid the bill.

But, in the end, the shock was Cory's.

They arrived at Blundham after a leisurely drive through narrow lanes. On the face of it the village, with its winding main street lined with pink-washed cottages, looked much the same. She recognised most of the names above the shops, and the pub, which had been rather run down, had received a much needed facelift, with window boxes, smart paintwork, and a new sign. It all had the same rather sleepy, prosperous air that she remembered.

'Why are there so many pink houses?' Rome queried, as he slowed for the corner.

Cory shook her head. 'It's just a traditional thing. You'll see it everywhere in Suffolk.' She pulled a face. 'My grandfather told me that originally they mixed the plaster with pigs' blood to get that particular colour, but I don't know if it's true or if he was just winding me up.' She leaned forward eagerly. 'If you take the left-hand fork down here, it will bring us to the house.'

'Who does it belong to now?'

'A London couple. He was something in the City, and she wanted to play the country lady.' Cory frowned slightly. 'I didn't like them much, and nor did my grandfather. He said they'd find it too big, and too isolated. In fact, he told them so, and the agents were furious. But they came up with the asking price, so they got it.'

Rome said slowly, 'Only it seems they didn't keep it.'

He brought the car to a halt beside a big estate agency sign attached to the front wall with 'Sold' blazoned across it.

And, in smaller letters, 'Acquired for the Countrywide Hotel Group.'

'A hotel. Oh, no, I don't believe it.' Cory sat for a moment, rigid with dismay, then scrambled out of the car. She peered through the tall wrought-iron gates. 'They haven't just sold it, they've actually moved out and left it empty. Look—the garden's like a jungle.'

She pushed at one of the gates, and it opened with a squeal of disuse.

'Countryside Hotels came sniffing around when we put the house on the market, but Gramps turned them down flat. He wanted it to remain a private home. That's why he sold to the Jessons.' She shook her head. 'I can't tell him. He'll be so upset.'

'Perhaps not,' Rome said quietly as he followed her up the overgrown drive. 'After all, he said it himself. Too big and too isolated. Maybe the Jessons gave it their best shot.' He put a hand on her shoulder. 'Cory, are you sure you wish to do this? Shall we go back to the car and drive up the coast?'

Her voice was subdued. 'We've come all this way. So I may as well say goodbye. And it could be worse,' she added, with a forced smile. 'It could have been bought by Sansom Industries and pulled down.'

She was half expecting a question or a comment, but Rome said nothing. Just gently removed his hand as they walked on towards the house.

It was redbrick, built on three storeys, with tall chimneys and mullioned windows.

'It's a good house,' Rome said, as they walked round to the rear. 'Simple and graceful. It doesn't deserve to be empty.'

'My room was up there. The window on the end.' Cory pointed. 'I chose it because at night I could hear the sound of the sea. Usually it was gentle and soothing, but when there were storms it would roar, and Gramps said it was a monster, eating back the land.'

'Didn't that give you nightmares?' Rome asked drily.

'No.' She shook her head decisively. 'Because I knew I was safe and loved. And the monster would never reach me.'

Or not then, she thought, with a pang. Her nightmare had begun with Rob...

'What's wrong?'

She started almost guiltily. Rome was watching her, frowning a little.

'Nothing—why?' She forced a smile.

'Your face changed,' he said. 'One moment you were remembering. The next you looked sad—almost scared.'

Cory paused. Shrugged. She said quietly, 'Maybe Memory Lane is a dangerous place.'

His mouth twisted. 'You think the future holds more security?' There was an odd note in his voice—almost like anger.

No, she thought with sudden desolation. Not if it holds you...

She said quietly, 'I try to live one day at a time—and not look too far ahead.'

She moved off determinedly along the stone terrace. 'Now I'll show you my grandmother's sunken garden. She used to grow roses there, and the most marvellous herbs.'

She reached the top of the stone steps and stopped dead, drawing a swift painful breath. Because the garden, with its tranquil paths and stone benches, had gone. In its place was a swimming pool, surrounded by an expanse of coloured tiles. Even the old summer house had been supplanted by a smart changing pavilion.

Cory's throat tightened. She turned and looked up into Rome's cool, grave face.

She said, like a polite child, 'Thank you for bringing me here, but I've seen enough and I'd like to go home, please.'

Then her face crumpled and she began to weep, softly and uncontrollably, the tears raining down her pale face.

Rome said something quiet under his breath. Then his arms went round her, pulling her close. His hand cradled her head, pressing her wet face into the muscular comfort of his chest.

She leaned against him, racked by sobs. He smelt of fresh air and clean wool, and his own distinctive maleness, a scent that seemed at the same time alien and yet totally familiar. She breathed him, filled herself with him, as her hands clung to his shoulders, her fingers twisting feverishly in the fine yarn of his sweater.

As she cried, he murmured to her, sometimes in English but mostly in Italian. While she didn't understand everything he said, instinct told her they were words of endearment, words of comfort.

And she felt his lips brush her hair.

She lifted her head and looked up at him, a sob still catching her throat, her eyes bewildered—wondering.

The long fingers touched her drenched lashes, then gently stroked her cheek, pushing back the strands of dishevelled hair. And all the time she watched him silently.

She felt him straighten, as if he was going to put her away from him, and whispered, 'Please...'

For a moment he was still. Taut. The dark face was stark, the blue eyes narrowed, suddenly, and burning.

And when he moved it was to draw her close again. But not, this time, for consolation.

He kissed her forehead, then, very softly, her eyes, as if he was blotting her tears with his lips.

She sighed, her body bending like a willow in his arms in a kind of mute offering. And then, and only then, he found her mouth with his.

She was more than ready. She was thirsting, starving for him. Her lips parted, welcoming the heated thrust of his tongue. Their mouths tore at each other in a kind of frenzy. She forgot to think, to reason, or to be afraid. There was nothing—*nothing*—but this endless kiss. This was what she'd been born for, and what she would die for if need be, she told herself, her brain reeling.

When he lifted his head at last, she was shaking so violently she would have collapsed but for his arm, like an iron bar, under her back.

He said her name swiftly, harshly, then bent his head again. He was more deliberate this time, more in control, his lips exploring her wet cheeks, the hollow of her ear and the leaping pulse in her throat, lingering there as if he was tasting the texture of her skin.

Then he kissed her lips again, fitting his mouth to hers with sensuous precision, letting his tongue play with hers, teasing her lightly, wickedly, into uninhibited response.

His free hand slid inside her sweater and moved upwards, pushing the encumbering folds away and seeking the soft mound of her breast. Stroking her gently, feeling the aroused nipple hardening against his palm under the thin camisole she wore, as she arched against him.

He lifted his head and stared down at her for a long moment, his eyes slumberous, urgent, as he studied the effect of his caress.

For a moment she returned his gaze, then her lashes swept down, veiling her eyes, as she waited for him to touch her again.

This time she experienced the shuddering thrill of his mouth against her, suckling her scented, excited flesh through the silk covering. Circling the rosebud peak with his tongue, coaxing it to stand proud against the damp and darkened fabric.

Cory could feel the heat of him—the male hardness—against her thighs in implicit, primitive demand, and heard herself moan swiftly and uncontrollably in need and surrender.

It was a small sound, but it broke the spell. Snapped the web of sensuality which held them.

Between one instant and the next Cory found herself released—free. And Rome standing three feet away from her, trying to control his ragged breathing.

He said quietly, as if speaking to himself, 'I did not—intend that.'

Hands shaking, Cory dragged her sweater back into a semblance of decency.

She said, in a voice she barely recognised, 'It was really my fault. You got—caught up in an overspill of emotion, that's all.'

'No,' he said harshly. 'It was entirely mutual. Have the honesty to admit it.'

There was a tense silence. Cory looked down at the flagstones. 'Are you—sorry it happened?'

'No—but I should not have allowed it, just the same.' He sounded weary, and a little angry. 'We had better go.'

She was still trembling as they walked back to the car. Her lips felt tender—swollen—and she touched them with a tentative finger.

'Did I hurt you?' He noticed, of course.

'No,' she said.

But it was a lie.

Because in those brief rapturous moments in Rome's

arms she had given him the power to hurt her for all eternity.

And eternity, she realised painfully, might already have begun.

CHAPTER SEVEN

THE clouds had returned with a vengeance, and the North Sea was a sullen grey as they drove up the coast road.

There was silence inside the car, but not the companionable sort, born of long familiarity. The enclosed atmosphere simmered with tension, and some other element less easy to define.

Cory sat huddled into the passenger seat, staring rigidly at the white-flecked waves emptying themselves on to the banks of shingle.

She did not dare look at Rome, who was concentrating almost savagely on his driving.

The advance and retreat of the sea was like a symbol of her own life, she thought, pain twisting inside her. One moment she was being carried along on an inexorable tide of passion. The next she was abandoned, stranded. Left clinging to some inner emotional wreckage. And she wasn't sure how much more she could take.

Any student of body language, she thought, would take one look at her and say 'defensive'. But they didn't know the half of it. The faint lingering dampness of her camisole against her skin was an unwanted but potent reminder of the subtle plunder his lips had inflicted.

Her entire being was one aching throb of unsatisfied longing.

While being shut with him in this confined space was nothing less than torture.

She sat up with sudden determination.

'Could you stop the car, please?—I'd like to go for a

105

walk—clear my head.' She shot a swift, sideways glance at his set, remote profile. 'If that's all right,' she added.

'Of course,' he said coolly. 'It's a good idea.' He paused. 'Something we both need, perhaps.'

The wind was freshening, blowing in unpleasant gusts from the sea, and Cory took off the scarf knotted at her neck and struggled to tie it over her hair instead.

'May I help?' Rome came round the car to her side.

'No.' Her mouth was suddenly dry, her heart pounding as she thought of his fingers touching her hair, brushing against her throat. 'No, I can manage. Thank you.'

He shrugged on the russet jacket, his eyes hard. 'As you wish.'

He set off and she followed, picking her way across the sliding shingle, filling her lungs with the cold salt-laden air as she battled with the wind.

Apart from clusters of sea birds hunched at the edge of the sea, and a couple exercising a small dog in the distance, they had the long stretch of beach to themselves.

Rome strode ahead, apparently impervious to the chill of the wind, or the increasing dampness in the air, and Cory found she was struggling to keep up with him.

Hey, she wanted to shout. This is my environment, not yours. How dare you be so at home here, when I feel alienated of—a stranger...?

At the top of the shingle bank, the elderly hulk of a fishing boat had been left to end its days, and Rome paused in the shelter of its remaining timbers, shading his eyes as he stared out to sea, watching the progress of a solitary oil tanker on the horizon.

As she joined him breathlessly, he gave her an unsmiling glance. 'How are the cobwebs?'

'They didn't survive the first minute.' She leaned against

the bow of the boat, steadying her flurried breathing and attempting to rearrange her scarf.

Rome resumed his scrutiny of the tanker, his expression unreadable. Silence hung between them.

Eventually, Cory cleared her throat. She said, 'I think I owe you an apology.'

'For what happened between us earlier?' Rome shook his head. 'We must share any blame for that.'

'I didn't mean—the kiss.' And what a polite euphemism that was, she thought wryly, for all that had really gone on.

'What, then?' His mouth was hard and set.

She said steadily, 'For bursting into tears all over you. I'm not usually such a wimp—I hope. It was just such a shock. The village looked just the same, so I'd convinced myself that Blundham House would, too. That it would still be there waiting for me, caught in some time warp, and that all I had to do was show up.' She shook her head. 'Stupid, or what?'

'Unrealistic, perhaps. But I encouraged that by bringing you here. I should not have done so. I just—needed to get out of London, and I thought you did, too.' He was still staring at the horizon, and his voice was bitter with self-accusation. 'This whole day was a bad mistake.'

Hurt twisted inside her. She said quietly, 'Rome—we both lost our heads for a while. But it's no big deal, and it certainly isn't irretrievable.'

His laugh was brief and humourless. 'You don't think so?' He turned to look at her. 'Cory, you can't be that naïve. You must see it has changed everything.'

She tried to look into his eyes, but they were hooded, unfathomable.

She forced a smile. 'Perhaps I'm due for a change.'

'That,' he said, 'would be unwise.'

'Then maybe I'm just tired of being sensible,' she threw back. 'But if you're not—I can learn to live with it.'

His mouth tightened. '*Dio*, I wish it were that simple.'

Cory leaned her shoulder against the boat, needing its support suddenly.

She said huskily, 'Rome—is there some—some reason why we shouldn't be—together?'

She'd meant to say 'someone else', but found she couldn't speak the words aloud.

He said bleakly, 'Any number of reasons, *mia cara*. Do you wish me to list them for you?'

No, she thought with swift anguish. Because one of them could be another woman's name. And more than she could bear.

That damned scarf was slipping again. She untied it, thrusting it into the pocket of her raincoat, glad to conceal the fact that her hands were shaking.

She said in a low voice, 'And what if I said I didn't care? That I want to forget the past and live just for the present?' She bit her lip. 'And let the future take care of itself.'

There was a tingling silence. Cory could almost feel the tension emanating from him.

He said, 'You don't know what you're saying, Cory. And you deserve better than that. You deserve a future.' He flung back his head in sudden anger. 'Dear God—what an unholy mess.'

She could taste blood from her ravaged lip. 'Then—again—I'm sorry. And I'll have to stop saying that.'

She looked past him at the sea, iron-dark now, like the sky above it. Saw a cloud advancing across the water, whipping up the surface like cream.

She said, 'We should get back to the car. There's a squall coming.' She added carefully, 'And, however it's turned out, it was good of you to give me this day. I'll remember it always. But I don't think there should be any more of them. When we get back to London, we should say goodbye.'

He said harshly, 'You think that's possible?'

'No,' she said. 'Essential.'

And gasped as the sheet of rain she'd seen approaching arrived in an icy torrent which drenched them relentlessly within seconds.

Rome swore, and grabbed her hand. 'Run,' he ordered.

The rain swirled at them, driven viciously by the wind, as they stumbled back across the treacherous shingle, struggling to keep their footing. They were breathless and half blinded when they reached the car.

Rome thrust Cory into the passenger seat, then dived in beside her. They sat for a moment, listening to the roar of the wind and the fierce drumming of the rain on the car roof.

Rome reached into the glove compartment and produced a packet of tissues.

He said wryly, 'For the moment, this is the best I can offer.'

Cory used a handful of them to blot the worst of the moisture from her face and hands. But she could do little about her hair, which was sticking to her scalp, and even less about her soaked clothing, now adhering clammily to her skin.

Even her eyelashes were dripping, she thought ruefully.

And Rome was in no better state.

She said doubtfully, 'It might be quicker to go back by the motorway...'

'Perhaps,' he said, starting the car. 'But I have a better idea.'

They drove back the way they had come. After a mile or so, Rome turned down a narrow lane.

'Where are we going?' Cory was shivering.

'I saw a hotel signposted on the way here. I'd planned to take you there for tea. We'll use their facilities to get dry instead.'

'But we can't do that. They won't allow it.'

'We have no choice,' Rome told her coolly. 'And nor do they. If we drive back to London in this state, we're risking pneumonia.'

He drove in between two tall brick pillars and up a winding, tree-shaded drive.

Through the rivulets of water still running down the windscreen, Cory got an impression of a large creeper-clad building with lights blazing cheerfully from its mullioned windows.

Rome brought the car to a halt in front of the main entrance.

He said, 'Wait here, while I see what can be done.'

Her lips were still framing another protest when he disappeared, leaving her with the beat of the rain for company.

Peering out through the streaked and misty windows, she could see a number of other cars parked nearby, and this heartened her.

If the hotel was busy, it wouldn't want extra waifs and strays dropping in because they'd been caught in a storm, she thought, easing her wet skirt away from her legs with distaste.

But even if the hotel rolled out the red carpet for them, she still couldn't go in there. Not with Rome.

The journey back to London was going to be difficult enough, and she didn't want to prolong the remainder of her time in his company.

And spending even a few hours with him in a remote

country hotel was bound to force on them the kind of intimacy she could never risk again.

Pneumonia, she thought, would almost be preferable.

She was so deep in her own unhappy thoughts that she was unaware of Rome's return until her door was opened abruptly.

'They can take us.' He handed her a big coloured umbrella. 'The porter will show you where to go, while I park the car. And I'll even be the soul of chivalry and let you have the first hot bath.'

Cory stared at him. She said huskily, 'You mean you've reserved a room?'

'Naturally. We'll need some privacy while our clothes are being dried.'

She said fiercely, 'Our day out is over, Rome. I thought I'd made that clear. And I'm not signing off by joining you in some seedy hotel room that you rent by the hour.'

'By the night, actually. Although it's our own business how long we stay. And I've brought you here because we're both very cold and very wet. This is dire necessity, Cory, not some elaborate seduction ploy.'

Her face warmed. 'We can't stay here. I won't. It—it's out of the question.'

'Then you're asking the wrong questions. Cory—don't be difficult. It's still pouring with rain, and I'm getting soaked again.'

She said stubbornly, 'I want to go back to London.'

'You shall.' His tone was gritty. 'But first I intend to have a bath, some food, and my clothes dried and pressed by the hotel valet service. I don't think that's unreasonable.' He paused. 'However, if you prefer to stay here, alone and dripping, and making yourself ill in the process, that is entirely your own decision. But in that case be good enough not to give me your cold.'

He paused again. 'Don't argue any more, *carissima*. I would carry you in, but the staff might get the wrong impression and give us the bridal suite.'

Cory gave him a fulminating look, and left the car with as much dignity as she could assemble at short notice.

The porter, small, balding and jolly, awaited her. 'Good afternoon, madam, and welcome to Hailesand Hotel. What a shame about the weather.' He relieved her of the wet umbrella. 'We've put you in the Garden Suite, and it's just down here.'

Cory found herself squelching down a thickly carpeted corridor. The porter threw open the door at the end with a flourish.

'This is the sitting room, madam.' He bustled around lighting lamps. 'The main bedroom's through that door on the right, and the bathroom's opposite, with the other bedroom next to it. Not that you'll need it, of course, but it's nice for families.'

'Yes,' was all Cory could manage.

'I'll put a match to the fire, shall I? Make things cosier for you,' he added with satisfaction as flames began immediately to curl round the kindling in the dog grate. 'And if you leave your wet clothes in the bedroom the housekeeper will collect them for you. You'll find complimentary robes in the wardrobe, and plenty of nice toiletries in the bathroom, so just relax and make yourself at home.

'Your husband said you'd be wanting tea,' he threw back over his shoulder on the way to the door. 'Just ring down to the desk when you're ready and I'll bring it—and some more logs for the fire.'

'Thank you,' Cory said, feeling as if she'd been bowled over by a giant teddy bear.

'You're welcome, madam.' He twinkled at her, and went out, leaving Cory to the confusion of her own thoughts.

Her initial reaction was thankfulness that they were in a suite, and not a double room. So at least she'd be able to maintain some kind of distance from him during their brief stay, she told herself painfully.

Her second thought was that if they had to stay somewhere while their clothes dried, this would seem the perfect choice.

Even without the fire the room would have been cosy, she thought, viewing the thickly cushioned twin sofas with their chintz covers which flanked the fireplace.

There was a small round dining table in one corner, and a bookcase crammed with a tempting selection of paperbacks.

The walls were hung with watercolours of local scenes, and there were bowls of fresh flowers everywhere. Old fashioned French windows offered access to the gardens beyond. Or would when it wasn't lashing with rain, Cory amended, with another shiver. Which reminded her what she was there for.

She eased her feet out of her shoes and peeled off her sodden tights, then padded across to the bathroom.

As she ran hot water into the tub, adding a sachet of freesia bath oil for good measure, she realised the friendly porter hadn't exaggerated. The pretty basket of toiletries even had toothbrushes and paste.

The main bedroom was attractively decorated in blue, the faint severity of the tailored bedspread and plain drapes offset by a cream carpet lavishly patterned in forget-me-nots.

Was that a subtle hint? Corey wondered, as she stripped off her wet clothes and put on the smaller of the two cream towelling robes from the wardrobe. If so, it was unnecessary.

Eventually, she hoped—she prayed—she would be able

to put the events of these few enigmatic days behind her. But not yet.

She put her discarded garments in the linen laundry bag she found in a drawer, but decided she would rinse out her own undies and dry them quickly on a radiator.

The robe was a perfectly discreet cover-up, but she'd feel awkward and self-conscious being so nearly naked in front of Rome.

For her own peace of mind, she needed more than one layer, she thought, her mouth twisting.

She took the other robe into the sitting room and draped it over the arm of the sofa, where he would see it, and placed the laundry bag beside it.

Then she went to have her bath, carefully turning the little brass bolt on the door first.

She lay half submerged in the scented bubbles like a mermaid on a rock. Except she felt that she was the one being lured to her doom, she thought, letting the water lap softly over her breasts and gasping a little at the sensation.

She had never been so aware of her own body before, nor of its unexpected capacity for pleasure.

But then, she had never before felt such overwhelming physical desire for a man as she did for Rome.

Not even Rob, whom she'd believed she loved, had been able to arouse such a fierce, unbridled need in her.

Perhaps if he had things would have been different between them, she thought, biting her lip.

But all that dizzying, aching passion for Rome had to be counterbalanced by the questions about him that remained unanswered.

It troubled her that she still knew so little about him. It genuinely shocked her that she'd been on the point of giving herself to a man who was still virtually a stranger to her. And who—one day, one night—would walk away, back to his own life. Leaving her bereft.

So the wise thing was to step back herself before she was tempted again. Before any real harm was done.

One of the nuns at her convent school had lectured the girls regularly on avoiding 'occasions of sin'. And Sister Benedict would have placed Rome in that category without a second thought.

He was the occasion, the sin itself, and the ultimate need for repentance all united in one lethal package.

She knew the right thing was never to see him again, even if the anguish of it made her want to moan out loud.

But she wouldn't sit at home brooding about what might have been. She would stop being so selective—so reclusive. She would do as her grandfather wanted. She'd go out and meet people, and somehow, sooner or later, she would find someone who would make this deep, aching hollow inside her disappear.

It was just a matter of time.

She shampooed her hair, rinsed out her camisole, briefs and tights, and folded them in a towel over her arm.

She combed her wet hair back from her face, and took a long objective look at herself. The sleeked back hair left her no defences at all, and she was all eyes and cheekbones, and soft vulnerable mouth.

But she couldn't stay in here, as if she was clinging to sanctuary. Somehow she had to endure the next few hours—survive them. And to do that she had to confront the man in the next room, whether angel or demon. And she had to do it now.

She took a deep breath, then opened the bathroom door and went into the sitting room.

Rome was standing by the French windows, staring into the gathering darkness. He was bare-legged, and the sleeves of the robe were folded back, exposing muscular forearms. His skin looked very dark against the pale fabric.

He turned slowly and looked at her, his expression watchful, almost wary. She had the sense of strong emotion rigorously controlled. Of a battle that had been fought and won during her absence.

She had to resist an impulse to tighten the sash of her robe—to draw its lapels closer together.

Behave calmly, she adjured herself silently. Treat the situation as if it was normal. As if it's not a problem.

She said, 'I'm sorry I took so long.' Then, shyly, 'This—this is a lovely place. Log fires and tea on demand.'

He smiled faintly. 'Give me ten minutes, then order some.' He paused. 'Our clothes will be a couple of hours, so I had them bring us a dinner menu. We can eat here.'

'Oh.' She couldn't keep the note of dismay out of her voice, and his brows lifted mockingly.

'The restaurant demands smart casual dress, *cara*,' he drawled. 'I doubt we would qualify. Also, we might be a little conspicuous.'

She said, 'I was hoping we'd be on our way back to London before dinner.'

'How eager you are to be off,' Rome commented caustically. 'You have a date tonight, perhaps?'

Cory did not meet his gaze. 'No—just a life to get back to.'

He said softly, 'Ah, yes, of course.'

He walked across the room, heading for the bathroom. As he passed Cory he bent, so that his mouth was almost brushing the delicate curve where her neck joined her shoulder, and inhaled with frank appreciation.

He said, 'You smell—exquisite, *mia bella*. Like some rare flower.'

Her body stiffened with almost unbearable tension. She kept her voice level with an effort. 'Thank you.'

She remained where she was until she heard the click of the bathroom door signal that she was alone.

Then she moved, like an automaton, to one of the sofas, and sank onto the edge of it, staring at the flames that were leaping round the logs. Consuming them. Burning them out.

Knowing that this could happen to her, too.

She thought, Oh, God, I have to be careful—so careful.

And found herself wondering if it was not already too late…

CHAPTER EIGHT

ROME tossed the disposable razor into the waste basket and rinsed his face. As he reached for a towel he paused, staring at himself in the mirror above the basin, his eyes bleak with self-condemnation.

Yet he couldn't blame himself totally for the present situation, he argued. He wasn't responsible for the weather which had stranded them here.

And although he'd been desperate to get away from London and out of his grandfather's aegis, he hadn't planned to take Cory with him. Not at first.

'What's happening with the girl?' Matt had demanded on the telephone, not for the first time. 'Why aren't you seeing her?'

Rome's brows drew together. 'Are you having me watched?' he asked coldly.

'That's my business. I've made an investment in you, boy,' Matt barked. 'And I protect my investments.' He paused. 'You took her to dinner, I understand, and that's good. But why haven't you followed it up?'

'Because I want her to ask herself that,' Rome said levelly. 'I want her to miss me.'

'Or forget all about you,' Matt said contemptuously. 'You could lose all the ground you've won.'

'You should have used the hired stud.' Rome's tone was short. 'You'd have found him more amenable to orders. I do this my own way. That was the agreement.'

'Then do it faster,' his grandfather snapped. 'This delay

is costing me money. You'd better make some progress this weekend, or you'll be hearing from me again.'

Rome replaced his receiver with a thud, his mouth grim. The temptation to tell Matt Sansom to go to hell was almost overwhelming.

But he couldn't afford that—yet.

He had no plans to contact Cory until the middle of next week. He wanted her intrigued—seriously bewildered—and with her guard down.

He retrieved the hated dossier and glanced through it, wondering where she was and what she was doing. An item about the National Gallery caught his eye. It seemed to be one of her favourite weekend haunts, and instinct suggested that it might be the kind of place she'd choose if she was troubled about something. If…

When he actually found her there he expected to feel mildly elated that he'd been able to predict her movements—and her mood—with such accuracy. Instead, he felt winded—as if someone had punched him savagely in the gut. He found himself leaning against a doorframe, almost gasping for breath.

Even then he didn't intend to approach her. He was, he told himself, just checking. And she had no idea he was there, watching her. So it would be easy to slip away.

Only to find himself walking across to her, as if impelled by some unseen force.

He didn't mean to mention the Suffolk trip either. After all, it was just an idea, still in the planning stage. He was saving it for later, like the cherry on the cake. Proof of how caring he was, he derided himself.

So why had he suddenly found himself blurting it out? Almost hustling her out of the Gallery and to his car as if she might suddenly drift through his fingers and vanish?

He shook his head in exasperation.

He'd given way to a series of crazy impulses—and this was the result.

And then he'd compounded all previous errors by kissing her. And not the studied kiss he'd taken in the restaurant, which had been solely intended to rattle her. To teach her in one swift lesson how fragile that cool reserve of hers really was.

No, the truth was that he'd wanted to feel that soft mouth of hers trembling under his again. Had needed it with sudden desperation.

But he hadn't anticipated her body's shaken response—or that she'd—offer herself with such candour.

He still wasn't sure where he'd found the strength to pull back. Perhaps some lurking shred of decency had reminded him that sex was not on offer. His decision. And that he'd be taking her under false pretences. Which she didn't deserve.

He sighed impatiently—angrily.

Because, at the same time, a small hard voice in his head was telling him that he was a fool. That this was the perfect opportunity to fulfil his deal with Matt.

By dawn tomorrow, he thought cynically, he could persuade Cory to be his wife—or anything else he might ask of her.

And then he'd be done with his grandfather's machinations and free to get on with his own life. Off the hook.

Which was what he wanted.

All that he wanted.

He tossed the towel aside and reached for his robe, tying the belt firmly round his lean waist.

And all he had to do, he told himself, was walk back into the next room and take it.

Because nothing could be too high a price to pay for Montedoro—could it?

He looked back in the mirror, but this time all he could see in his eyes was confusion.

Cursing under his breath, he switched off the light and went into the sitting room.

Cory was curled up in a corner of one of the sofas, a magazine open on her lap which she was reading with elaborate concentration.

On the table in front of her was a tray of tea, newly arrived.

Rome halted, his mouth twisting involuntarily. He said softly, 'How very domestic.'

She looked up at him. Apart from a faint flush in her cheeks, she appeared totally composed.

She said sedately, 'Except that I don't know if you take milk and sugar.'

He stretched out on the opposite sofa, smiling at her. 'Just milk, please. But I like my coffee black.' He paused. 'Do you think you'll remember?'

Cory busied herself with the teapot. 'I can just about manage that—for one evening.'

She put the cup where he could reach it. Poured her own tea. Made a studied return to her magazine.

The room was silent but for the splash of rain on the windows and the crackling of the logs in the fireplace. The warmth had dried her hair, turning it into a silken cloud round her face.

One strand drifted across her cheek and she pushed it back, knowing, in spite of herself, that the small gesture had not been lost on him. That he was reading her with the same close attention that she was paying her magazine. And probably learning far more.

He said, 'I didn't know you played golf.'

'I don't.'

'Then why read a golfing magazine?'

'I—I'm thinking of taking it up,' she said defensively, and was immediately furious with herself for perpetrating such an obvious and ridiculous lie.

'You've come to the right place,' Rome said lazily. 'When I was registering, the place started heaving with frustrated and very damp golfers, all forced off the links by the weather.'

She'd hoped to use the magazine as a barricade, but clearly that wasn't going to work, so she tossed it aside.

She said, 'When do you think our clothes will be returned?'

He shrugged. 'What's the hurry?' He smiled again, his gaze tracing the open neckline of her robe. 'I like you better the way you are.'

Cory bit her lip. 'I don't,' she said shortly, resisting an impulse to draw the lapels closer and tighten her sash. 'I'd prefer to be dressed and out of here.'

'Don't hold your breath,' Rome advised with a shrug. 'I gather this is a hotel that prides itself on service. Our clothes will be brought back when they're ready, and not a moment earlier.'

Cory studied him for a moment, frowning. 'It's odd,' she said, 'but sometimes you don't sound Italian at all.'

'There's nothing strange about it,' he said. 'I was accidentally born there. But I doubt that I have any genuine Italian blood.'

She said, 'But surely your mother...'

'My mother was English,' he said. 'She quarrelled with her family and ran off to Europe, and she happened to be in Rome when I was born. That's all.'

She said, 'Oh.'

He grinned sardonically. 'Disappointed, *cara*?' he challenged. 'Now that you know I can't be descended from del Sarto's model?'

She flushed. 'Don't be absurd. And please stop calling me *cara*,' she added with asperity.

'Then what shall I call you?' Arms folded behind his head, fingers laced, he regarded her. 'Darling—my love—my sweet?'

She did not look at him. 'No, thank you.'

'You make things very difficult.' He spoke softly, faint laughter in his voice. 'Italian is such a beautiful language for making love.'

'It's also just a pretence,' she said quietly. 'When you're not Italian.'

There was a silence, then, *'Touché,'* he murmured. 'Which I believe is French.' He paused. 'Does it matter so much—my not being Italian?'

'It doesn't matter at all. Except...'

'Tell me.'

She smoothed the towelling robe over her thigh. 'Except that I never seem to get to know you—know who you really are. Or what you want.'

Her voice lifted in a kind of appeal. She felt him hesitate, and waited.

But Rome's eyes were hooded. He said lightly, 'At the moment, my priority is dinner. Have you looked at the menu yet?'

'Yes.' Cory fought down her disappointment. Whenever she thought she was getting close to him, he retreated to a distance again. But why?

She cleared her throat. 'I thought—the pâté, followed by the beef in red wine.'

'That's what I'm having.' His voice was cool. 'And as we're clearly soulmates, you can stop wondering about me, *mia bella*—and worrying.'

But Cory, watching him rise lithely to his feet and cross

the room to telephone their order, knew it could never be that simple.

Because instinct was telling her that knowledge could be dangerous. And that sometimes it was better—and safer to go on wondering…

He said, 'Tell me about your grandmother.'

Dinner was over, and they were lingering over coffee. The food had been delicious, and, to Cory's surprise, Rome had ordered a bottle of dark, velvety wine to accompany their meal.

As he'd filled their glasses, she'd said doubtfully, 'Do you think that's wise?'

'You'd have preferred a Bordeaux?'

She'd said, 'I was thinking about later…' and had flushed when he'd raised his eyebrows and begun to laugh.

She'd said hurriedly, 'I meant you shouldn't drink and drive.'

'I'm disappointed.' He had still been grinning. 'But I promise to stay well within the limit,' he'd added softly. 'On all counts.'

Which, Cory thought, smouldering, had been enough to kill anyone's appetite stone dead.

Yet, strangely, she'd eaten every crumb of pâté, and done full justice to the rich and fragrant casserole. The wine, too, lingered on the palate.

Now, the table had been cleared by an efficient young waitress, and the tray of coffee she'd brought had been placed on the table by the fire.

Cory would have preferred to stay at the dining table, which had conferred a kind of much-needed formality to the proceedings.

She was listening all the time for the knock on the door which would announce the return of their clothing.

Her camisole and briefs had quickly dried on the bedroom radiator, and she was now wearing them again under her robe. They were only a fragile form of protection at best, but she felt better—safer with them on.

But she wouldn't really relax until she had the rest of her things back.

All through dinner she'd been taking surreptitious glances at her watch as she marked the way time was passing all too quickly.

If they didn't leave here soon, she thought, it might be too late...

Then mentally berated herself for being over-fanciful.

She had no real reason to feel threatened. Rome had been the perfect dinner companion, chatting with her on all kinds of topics, sounding out her opinions, even arguing lightly at times.

So far the conversation had been general. But now Rome's question about Beth had moved it back to the personal again.

She moved restively. 'My grandmother? Why do you want to know?'

'Because the two of you were clearly close, and I'm interested.' He paused. 'Does it hurt you to talk about her?'

Cory's smile was suddenly tender. 'No, not really. She was just a lovely person—very gentle, and calm, and she and my grandfather adored each other. She told me once it was love at first sight—although when they met she was actually engaged to someone else.'

'Who also, presumably, found her gentle and lovely.' Rome grimaced. 'It must have been a bitter pill for him to swallow.'

'Yes,' Cory admitted. 'But Gran had already realised they weren't right for each other. She was going to break off the engagement anyway. Meeting Gramps was just the final impetus she needed.'

'And what about you?' Rome said. 'Do you believe in love at first sight?'

She drank some coffee. She said, 'I suppose there has to be a real initial attraction in any relationship. But on the whole I think love should build up from trust—friendship—respect.'

'How very virtuous,' he said softly. 'And what about passion—desire—the touch of someone's hand that tells you the world has changed for ever? Does that mean nothing?' He paused. 'Or is that what scares you?'

This, she thought, was what she'd been dreading from the first.

He didn't have to put a hand on her. This line of questioning could strip her naked emotionally.

The atmosphere in the room seemed to have thickened suddenly—become electrically charged. The heat from the burning logs had become too intense. The brush of the towelling robe against her bare skin was almost more than she could endure.

She said, too vehemently, 'I'm not scared.' And wondered precisely whom she was trying to convince.

'Then why won't you look at me?'

Somehow, she made herself lift her head. Meet his gaze.

His mouth was smiling faintly, making her remember how it had felt on hers. His eyes were caressing her—pulling away the thick enveloping folds of the robe. Uncovering her, she thought dizzily, for his private delight.

He hadn't laid a finger on her, but the mere possibility had the power to make her body moisten and melt. And he had to be aware of it. Had to know what he was doing to her...

And she had no defences. Technically, she wasn't a virgin. Her brief time with Rob had dealt with that on a physical level. But sensually, and emotionally, she was untouched. And she knew it. As he must, too.

She said swiftly, huskily, *'Don't...'*

'Why not?'

She could think of a host of reasons, including all the high-flown phrases about respect and trust that she'd already trotted out.

But they all seemed unimportant against the burning reality of need. It was crude and it was violent, and it was tearing her apart. So that all she could do was stare at him wordlessly—and wait.

He said again, quietly, 'Why not?'

And this time it was an affirmation of a decision already made. A pact that had been agreed.

The tap at the door was a jolt to her senses as sudden and shocking as a blow, so that she almost cried out.

Rome got to his feet and went to the door. She heard a murmur of voices, and then the porter was there with their clothes, beautifully pressed under plastic covers, draping them carefully over the arm of a sofa.

She thought, My reprieve. And part of her wanted to laugh hysterically, while the other half wanted to cry...

She heard a stranger using her voice, thanking him, and asking him politely to take the coffee tray away.

'Certainly, madam. Is there anything else I can get you this evening—or your husband?'

And heard Rome say, 'No, that's fine. We have everything we need, thanks. Goodnight.'

She found she was repeating the words 'everything we need' over and over in her head.

When Rome came back to the sofa, she began to babble. 'They think we're married. Even though I'm not wearing a ring.' She spread out bare hands. 'See. Isn't that absurd?'

'Ludicrous,' he said, and his voice was very quiet.

'And you were right,' she hurried on. 'They've made a really good job of the valeting. Everything looks as good as new. And I reckon if we hurry we can still be back in London before midnight...'

Her voice tailed off with a gasp as Rome knelt in front of her, taking her shaking hands in his and holding them.

He said gently, 'Cory, we're not going anywhere tonight. You know it, and so do I, so let's stop pretending.'

She heard herself say in a voice she hardly recognised, 'Yes.'

He got to his feet, drawing her up with him, then lifted her into his arms as if she were some tiny featherweight and carried her into the bedroom.

The big shaded lamps were burning on each side of the bed, and the cover had been turned back. Rome put her down gently against the pillows and came to lie beside her. She was trembling, but she made no protest as he undid the sash of her robe and parted its folds.

He looked at her for a long moment, the dark face arrested, intent. Then he said huskily, *'Mia bella.'* He raised her slightly, freeing her arms from the encumbering sleeves, then dropped the robe on to the floor beside the bed.

The long fingers trailed slowly across the swell of her breasts above the lace edging of her camisole, then cupped her chin, lifting her face for his kiss.

Her lips parted on a small sigh, welcoming him. The pressure of his mouth was slow and sweet as it explored hers, while his hands began their own journey of conquest, stroking the length of her slender body in one considered act of possession.

The silk she was wearing shivered against her skin at his touch. She felt him ease the camisole upwards, and closed

her eyes as he drew it gently from her body and discarded
it.

The room was warm, but she was suddenly cold, turning
on to her side away from him, wrapping her arms round
her body.

He put his arm round her, pulling her back against him,
and she realised he was naked. And not merely naked, but
deeply and powerfully aroused.

Rome put his lips against her throat, just below her ear,
making the tell-tale pulse leap to the brush of his mouth.
His fingers shaped the curve of her shoulder, and she trem-
bled like a frightened bird under his hand.

He kissed her throat again, and the sensitive nape of her
neck, moving the silky tendrils of hair aside with his lips.

He whispered coaxingly, 'Take your hands away, *mia
cara*. Don't hide from me. I want to know everything about
you.'

'There isn't a great deal to learn.' She tried to make a
joke of it, but her voice was too small and too breathless.

'Oh, you're so wrong,' he told her softly. 'I have to find
out what you like.' He let his lips travel down her throat
to the delicate hollow at its base. 'And what you may not
like.' He ran a tantalising finger down the centre of the
back she kept turned to him, making her flinch and gasp.
His hand moved round, closing on her hip for a moment,
then drifting down to her slender thigh, where it lingered,
warm, sensuous and quite deliberate.

'And what you might enjoy if you tried,' he whispered.

Her whole body seemed to shudder. Then she twisted
away from him, swiftly, almost violently.

She said in a suffocated voice. 'I—I can't do this. I
thought—but I can't.'

Rome stayed still for a long moment, his eyes fixed
thoughtfully on the long, vulnerable line of her back. Then

he moved, too, taking the pillows and piling them up behind him. He reached for her, ignoring the small stifled sound she made, and drew her back beside him, holding her in the crook of his arm with her face against his shoulder.

He pulled the sheet over them, covering himself to the waist and tucking the embroidered hem across her breasts.

He said, 'Is that less threatening?'

She said on a sigh, 'I suppose.' She hesitated. 'You must think I'm a terrible fool.'

He dropped a kiss on her hair. 'Don't try to read my thoughts,' he told her gently. 'Because you're way off target.'

'Don't you—mind?'

'I'm disappointed, of course,' he said. 'But, ultimately, the decision was always yours to make.' He paused, allowing her to digest that. 'However, I'd be interested to know why you changed your mind. If you can tell me.'

There was a charged silence, then she sighed again, a small desolate sound.

She said, 'You've seen how clumsy I am. I can hardly walk across a room without falling over my feet, or someone else's.'

'I saw you fall once because you were startled,' he said. 'That's all, and scarcely a federal case.'

'It's not all,' she threw at him. 'I'm also too tall, too skinny, and my feet are too big.'

He said, 'If we're listing faults, my nose is too large, I'm seriously bad-tempered until I get my coffee in the mornings, and I sing in the shower even though I can't.'

She said passionately, 'Don't laugh at me. This isn't a joke.'

He said slowly, 'No, I see that. But even if all those

claims you make are true, why should that stop you making love with me?'

She buried her face in his shoulder. Her voice came to him muffled. 'Because I—honestly can't do it. I'm—useless in bed. A—a freak. I can't bear you to know it, too.'

His breath caught in sheer astonishment. His hand cupped her chin, forcing her to look at him.

He said roughly, 'What is this nonsense? Never let me hear you say such things again.'

'Even when it's the truth?'

'And everything else is an act?' Rome shook his head. 'I don't believe that, Cory. Not when I've kissed you—felt your body come alive in my arms.'

She said with difficulty, 'It isn't the—wanting. It's what comes afterwards.'

He said quietly, 'Didn't you hear what I said just now—that I want to find what makes you happy?'

'But I need to make you happy, too,' she said. 'And I can't.'

Rome stroked the curve of her white, unhappy face with a gentle finger.

He said, 'I'm really not that hard to please, *mia cara*.'

She said on a whisper, 'But I wouldn't want you to be kind either—or to make allowances.' She thought with a pang of anguish, or laugh about me afterwards...

There was a silence, then he said, 'Who was he, Cory? The man who made you like this? Because there must have been someone, and I need to know all of it.'

He felt her shudder again. She said, 'Please, I don't want to talk about it.'

His hand gentled the line of her jaw, traced her throat and shoulder.

He said, 'But you need to be rid of it, *mia*, before it poisons your whole life. So, you must tell me...'

She was quiet for a while, then she said, 'We were going to be married. His name was Rob, and he worked for a merchant bank in the City. I—I'd been at school with his sister. I hadn't liked her much then, but I'd run into her a couple of times in London afterwards, and she was much friendlier. She even invited me to her birthday party.'

'And you met him there?'

'Yes. He spent a lot of time with me. I'm not much of a dancer, so we sat out on the terrace and talked. He—seemed to like all the things I did, but I realised later that Stephanie must have primed him. He phoned the next day, invited me to dinner. It was a wonderful two months,' she added stiltedly. 'We went everywhere together, and then he asked me to marry him. I suppose he—swept me off my feet.'

The arm that held her was like a band of iron.

'Go on,' Rome said tersely.

'But although we spent all that time together, we weren't lovers. Oh, he'd tried, but I—I suppose I wanted to wait until we were married. Then one evening, a few weeks before the wedding, we were having dinner at his flat, and it seemed silly to go on saying no.'

'So, you went to bed with him?'

'Yes.' Her throat tightened uncontrollably. 'I was incredibly naïve, but I just didn't expect it to be like that—so painful and so—quick. I was in love with him, for God's sake, and I didn't feel a thing. I just wanted it to be over.

'When we did it again, I tried to respond—to do what he wanted. I could sense he was disappointed, getting impatient, and that hurt in a different way.' She paused. 'After that I—pretended to be asleep.

'When I woke up in the morning, he wasn't there, and I supposed he'd gone off to make some coffee. I just wanted to leave—get back to my own place and have a shower.

I—I felt dirty somehow—and confused. It was as if Rob had suddenly become a different person—and one I wasn't sure I liked.

'He had a phone extension beside his bed. I picked it up to phone for a cab and realised he was on the line in the living room—talking—laughing to some friend.

'He said, "I tell you, man, bed's going to be a nightmare. She hasn't a bloody clue, and it's like making love to a coathanger anyway. I'll just have to keep my eyes shut and think of all that lovely money."'

She felt Rome move swiftly and restively beside her. She risked a swift glance upwards and saw his face, bleak and set, his eyes staring in front of him as if fixed by some troubled inner vision.

She said, 'For a moment I tried to pretend it wasn't me he was talking about. I couldn't believe he could be so cruel. I knew I hadn't been—any good that night, but he'd told me that I'd learn—and it would get better.'

'Then he lied.' Rome's voice was harsh. 'It would never have been any better for you, Cory. Not with him.'

She said, 'I realised for the first time that he'd never actually cared about me at all. That it had just been an act. I got dressed, and left. I could hardly bear to look at him, but I told him that it was all off. That there would be no wedding and I never wanted to see him or hear from him again.'

She shuddered. 'He got so angry then, and started shouting at me. Telling me I was making a fool of him—of myself, and what made me think anyone else would ever want me, no matter how much money I had. I could hear him all the way down the corridor to the lift. People were opening their doors—staring at me. I—I wanted to die.

'The wedding was cancelled. I told Gramps that I'd changed my mind, but I never told him why. I—I couldn't.

I've never told anyone—until now. Everyone—even my best friend—assumed he'd been unfaithful, and I let them think so. It was—less painful, somehow.'

There was silence, then Rome moved abruptly. Reaching for his robe, he said, 'I need a drink. Can I get you one?'

She shook her head. 'No—thanks.' But her heart cried out, Don't leave me—stay with me.

Even though she knew it was impossible, and that one day soon Rome would go from her life for ever.

Leaving her, she realised, a stifled sob rising in her throat, more bereft that Rob ever had, or could have.

Condemning her to spending the rest of her life alone—and lonely.

CHAPTER NINE

ROME closed the bedroom door carefully behind him and leaned against it, his breathing as hard and strained as if he'd taken part in some marathon.

Saying he wanted a drink had just been an excuse. Suddenly he'd needed to be on his own—to think. To come to terms with what he'd just heard. If he could...

He walked over to the French windows, opened them and gulped the chill rain-washed air into his lungs.

He felt nauseous—sick to his stomach. And dizzy with the kind of shame that no amount of alcohol could cure.

The decent thing, he knew, would be to get dressed and take Cory home before he did more harm.

She might be hurt, but that was inevitable. And it was nothing compared with the wound he would almost certainly inflict if they stayed together.

As he'd listened to her struggling with the quiet, halting story, he'd been possessed with a savage longing to seek out this unknown Rob and give him the beating of his life.

Except, as he'd suddenly realised, he was no better. For wasn't he deceiving Cory just as viciously—and for money?

Cursing under his breath, he leaned against the doorframe, staring up at the scudding clouds.

He was caught in this trap, and there was no escape. Whatever he did, the end result would be the same.

He would lose her.

He wasn't sure of the precise moment when she'd become essential to him, or how it had happened—or why.

He only knew that when he'd gone to her in the Gallery that morning it had been because he couldn't keep away any longer. He'd been drawn to her, instinctively, involuntarily, knowing that he had to be with her, whatever the eventual cost.

He hadn't, he thought wryly, even had a chance to fight it. In too deep before he knew it, and lost for ever.

Yet there was no way they could ever be together. This was the brutal reality he had to face. The anguish that twisted in his gut.

If he told her the truth she would turn from him in hurt and disgust. And even if he could prevail upon her by some miracle to trust him again he would have nothing to offer her. Because Montedoro—his home, his livelihood—would have gone. He would be starting again with bare hands, and he couldn't ask any woman to share that kind of hardship, even if she were willing.

While if he simply continued with his grandfather's plan, let the whole thing run its treacherous course, she would end up betrayed and—hating him.

But no more, he thought wearily, than he hated himself.

He stepped back into the room and closed the windows. He collected a bottle of mineral water from the bar, and two glasses, and took them back into the bedroom.

Cory had not moved. Her eyes were closed, but he knew she wasn't asleep.

And she'd been crying. He could see the marks on her face, and felt the hard knot of reason inside him dissolve into an aching tenderness and, a heartbeat later, into a need that could not be denied any longer.

To hell with the right thing, he thought, shrugging off his robe, letting it drop to the carpet. They would have this one night together. A chance, perhaps, for him to undo the harm that Rob had done and prove to her that she was a woman both desirable and capable of desire.

Maybe his last chance.

While, for a few hours, he in his turn could forget shoddy bargains, threatened ruin, and the inevitability of heartbreak, and think instead of nothing but her. Lose himself completely in the slender paradise of her body.

He slid into bed beside her, and drew her gently back into his arms. Her eyelids fluttered and she looked at him, her eyes wide and bewildered.

She said, 'Rome...' and he laid a quieting finger on her lips.

'Hush, *mia cara*,' he whispered. 'Don't speak. Just— feel.'

And he began to kiss her.

Even as her lips parted beneath his, Cory knew she should resist. But the urge to yield was too strong, too beguiling, she realised dazedly.

His skin smelt cold and fresh, as if he'd been in the open air, and she wanted to ask him about it, only other ideas, other sensations were beginning to press on her, driving coherent thought away.

His hands seemed to drift on her, and everywhere they touched her skin sang. She felt her body lift, arching towards him in a silent demand which was almost pleading.

He pushed away the concealing sheet and caressed her breasts slowly and very gently, making the rosy nipples soar in proud response. He bent his head, worshipping each small, delicate mound in turn with his lips, letting his tongue flicker over the aroused peaks, forcing a small, frantic sound from her throat.

His mouth returned to hers, soothing her. Whispering

softly in Italian against her lips, coaxing her to relax—to trust…

The fingers that stroked her skin were warm and leisurely, exploring every curve, every plane and angle as they moved downwards, and she felt his touch in her veins, quickening her bloodstream.

When his hand reached the silken barrier of her briefs she tensed again, and Rome paused, running a questing finger along the band of lace that circled her hips.

He kissed her more deeply, the play of his tongue against hers a heated, wicked incitement.

His lips moved to the whorls of her ear, and down to the haywire pulse in her throat.

The hot dart of his tongue penetrated the valley between her breasts, licking the salty excited moisture from her skin.

His cheek rested against her ribcage, assimilating the flurried thud of her heartbeat, and his hand moved downwards with exquisite deliberation, his fingertips burning through that final fragile barrier, but so slowly that she thought she might not be able to bear it.

Because she knew where she needed him—where she craved him—and he was making her wait—dear God—so long. So terribly—agonisingly long.

Her thighs were slackening and parting, offering him access in a molten, scalding rush.

He touched her through the silk, grazing softly, intimately against her tiny, excited bud. Then delicately increasing the pressure, using that last covering against her to deepen the delicious friction. Creating a rhythm that she could recognise—that she could respond to.

The breath caught in her throat as she lifted her hips to thrust herself against his hand in open need. To tell him that she wanted that ultimate obstacle gone—to be as naked as he was himself.

Suddenly Cory could feel the velvet hardness of him against her thigh. Her hand cupped him shyly, marking him, measuring him. She heard him groan softly in answer.

He moved swiftly then, stripping away her final defence, his fingers reclaiming her with total mastery. Stroking her, circling on her, drawing her into a sudden breathless spiral of sensation. Bringing her with throbbing intensity closer and closer to some undreamed-of edge where all control would be gone.

This was uncharted territory, and for a moment she was scared, afraid of ceding him too much. Of losing her identity and becoming some mindless creature of his instead.

And, as if he sensed her sudden tension, she heard him whisper against her skin, 'Don't fight me, *cara*. Come with me.'

His hand moved again, and almost at once she was lost, crying out soundlessly, wordlessly, as her body was caught—tossed to heaven and back—in the rippling convulsions of her first orgasm.

And Rome held her close and kissed her, and felt her shocked, delighted tears on his lips.

When she spoke, her voice was husky, dreaming. She said, 'I never knew—I never guessed...'

She felt his smile against her hair as she lay, her head pillowed on his chest.

He said, 'And that's only the first lesson.'

'What's the second?'

'This.' He took her hand and brought it gently to his body again.

'Ah.' Her fingers encircled him, softly, teasingly. Caressed him with new knowledge—new wonder. And, she realised, new confidence, as she felt him stir beneath her touch. 'And only this?'

Rome said thickly, 'No.'

He turned, tangling a hand in her dishevelled hair, bringing her mouth to his powerfully and urgently while his other hand began a long journey down the length of her spine, tracing the curve of her hip and the taut roundness of her buttocks with sensuous greed.

Cory found herself shivering with pleasure under the passage of the long, clever fingers, her body arching—straining towards him—so that the sensitive points of her breasts grazed the hard wall of his chest.

She said breathlessly, 'I want you. All of you.'

'Show me.' The invitation was almost a challenge, delivered huskily.

She felt the heat, the potency of him at the apex of her thighs, and, gasping, driven by pure instinct as her body melted—opened, she brought him into her.

He entered her slowly, his control absolute, the blue eyes scanning hers for any sign of pain or fear. But her gaze was clouded, sultry with pleasure, her breathing quickening with excitement as his strength filled her.

Then, when the union of their bodies was complete, he held her for a long moment, giving her time to accustom herself to this new sensation. Waiting…

Her hands touched his shoulders, revelling in their hard muscularity. Her fingers stroked the dark silky hair at the nape of his neck. She placed her hands flat against his chest, feeling the hammer of his heartbeat, revealingly unsteady, against her palms.

Her finger brushed his lips and he captured it, biting gently at the soft flesh.

Then, gently but deliberately, Cory began to move under him, and he matched her, taking her rhythm, letting her dictate the pace. Carefully reining back his own need for release for her pleasure.

Her body rose and fell, answering his measured thrusts. Glorying in them.

He kissed her mouth, his tongue hot and demanding against hers, then the arch of her neck, and the small eager breasts, suckling the hard pink nipples, making her moan in her throat, her head turning restlessly on the pillow.

He was murmuring to her against her flesh, his voice slurred and heavy.

Nothing existed for her in the universe but this man, in her bed, in her arms, in her body. She buried her face against him, breathing him, wanting to be absorbed into him.

His hand slipped down between them to the moist centre of her, softly and sensually caressing, and she felt the first quiver of rapture rippling like water across her being.

She lifted her legs, clasping them round his lean hips, her hands clinging to his shoulders as Rome began to drive more deeply, more powerfully, inciting her, drawing her on.

She said something—sobbed something that might have been his name—and found herself overtaken, her body imploding, fragmenting into ecstasy.

She cried out wildly, eyes blind, all her senses consumed by pleasure, and he answered her, his body juddering dangerously in his own climax.

Afterwards, when the world had steadied to a semblance of reality, they were very quiet together, lying close, kissing softly.

She said wonderingly, 'I thought I was dying.'

'They call it the little death.' There was a smile in his voice. 'Do you want me to prove that you're still very much alive?'

She looked at him demurely from under her lashes. 'You think you could?'

'Not at this moment, perhaps.' He grinned at her lazily. 'But soon.'

She was silent for a moment. 'Rome—is it—always like that?'

'It was like it for us,' he said. 'Isn't that all that matters?'

'Yes.' Her voice was quiet. 'Thank you.'

'For what?'

'For the lessons—all of them.' She forced a smile. 'I think I've just undergone a crash course. And I'll always be grateful.'

He propped himself on an elbow and looked down at her. He said slowly, 'What we had just now was beautiful, and sensational, and totally mutual—as you must know. So gratitude doesn't enter into it.'

She played with the embroidered edge of the sheet. 'But it's not the same for you. It can't be. You can't possibly pretend it was your first time...'

He took her hand and carried it to his lips. He said, 'It was my first time with you, Cory. And you blew my mind. And if you've got it into your head that I made love to you out of sympathy, I have to tell you I'm not that altruistic.'

She said, not looking at him, 'Would you have made love to me if I hadn't told you about Rob?'

'You hadn't told me about Rob when we walked home from Alessandro's—and I could barely keep my hands off you.' His voice was cool and considering. 'Nor at Blundham House this afternoon. We went up in flames together, Cory, and you know it. We could fight it as much as we liked, but it was really only a matter of time before we ended up in bed with each other.'

He paused. 'But, in the interests of frankness, I'll admit I wanted to make it good for you so that it would drive

that poisonous bastard out of your mind, once and for all.'
He framed her face with his hands, speaking very distinctly.
'He can't damage you any more, *carissima*, do you under-
stand? He's gone—finished with—so forget him.'

He dropped a kiss on her nose. 'Are you hungry?'

A gurgle of laughter welled up inside her. She said,
'That's quite a change of subject.'

'Not really,' he said. 'Because I no longer have to fight
to keep my hands off you, and the time is fast approaching
when it won't be enough for me to simply look at you and
talk to you.'

He kissed her mouth softly and sensuously.

'We have a long night ahead of us, *mia bella*,' he whispered, 'and we need to keep our strength up. So—I'll ask
you again—are you hungry?'

And, to her own astonishment, she was.

Rome ordered smoked salmon sandwiches and champagne from Room Service, and she ate and drank, propped
up on pillows in the crook of his arm, and knew she had
never felt so happy or so much at peace.

The awkward girl, she told herself, had given way to a
woman with her own sexual power.

And then, like a frost to blacken her mood, came another
thought.

How in the world, she asked herself with anguish, was
she ever going to live without him?

He said, 'You're very quiet.'

Cory started slightly, banishing the unhappy reverie that
she'd conjured up some five minutes before. She said
lightly, 'Just conserving my energy.'

Rome took her chin between thumb and forefinger and
tilted her face so he could look into her eyes. 'Truly?'

'Of course,' she lied. 'Try me.'

His face was solemn, but his eyes were dancing. '*Mia cara*, I thought you would never ask. Just let me get rid of these plates.'

When he came back, his expression was oddly brooding, as if he too had been having unpleasant thoughts.

She said, 'Is something wrong?'

'I hope not.' He sat on the edge of the bed, studying her. 'But I don't know.' He was silent for a moment, then said abruptly, 'Cory, *mia*—are you on the Pill?'

'The Pill,' she repeated wonderingly, then grasped the implication. 'Oh.' She swallowed. 'No—no, I'm not. I—I never have been.'

'That,' Rome said grimly, 'is what I was afraid of.' He shook his head. 'Dear God, how stupid—how irresponsible can I be?'

She put a hand out to him. 'It's not your fault. I'm just as much to blame. I wasn't thinking...'

'Nor was I,' he said. 'But I should have been.' His tone was bitter with self-reproach. 'I should have taken care of you.'

She watched him in silence for a few moments. She said, her voice quiet, 'Would it matter so much—if it happened? If I was—pregnant?'

He said roughly, 'Cory—you're not a child. You know it would.'

She'd hoped for comfort, and instead there was pain. He was telling her, she realised, that they had no future together. That sex, however wonderful, was not enough to make a lasting relationship—and a baby would just be an unwanted, indeed an impossible complication.

And you, she thought, are all kinds of a fool to have hoped for anything different.

She found herself praying that she hadn't given herself

away too seriously, and wondering, at the same time, what she could do to retrieve the situation.

One thing she was sure of. If this was all she was to have of Rome, then she would make it memorable—for both of them.

She lay back against the pillows and smiled at him composedly. She said, 'If the horse is gone, there's little point in worrying about the stable door—is there? So why don't we do as we planned and—enjoy the rest of the night?'

He groaned. '*Carissima*—be sensible.'

She said softly, 'Oh, it's much too late for that.' She let the sheet fall away from her breasts. She heard the small sound he made in his throat, and her smile deepened. 'Besides—I'm getting impatient...'

Hours—perhaps aeons—later, she lay beside him as the early-morning light began to penetrate the room and watched him sleep. His breathing was deep and peaceful, his skin dark against the white bedlinen.

He deserved his rest, she thought, colour warming her face as she remembered how one act of love had seemed to flow naturally into the next. As she recalled the things he'd said to her—the things he'd done.

Their bodies had moved together with such harmony, she thought. There'd been laughter too, and, once, tears.

And now it was over.

Moving carefully, she slid out of bed, collected her clothing and went to the bathroom.

She looked in on him again before she left. He was still sleeping, but he'd moved into the space she'd vacated as if unconsciously seeking her.

The porter was not on duty when she went down to the foyer, but there was a friendly girl at the reception desk, who told Cory the nearest station with a direct link to

London, looked up the time of the next train, and ordered her a taxi to take her there.

'There's no need to disturb my husband,' Cory said calmly. 'He's planning to spend the day locally—do some walking. But unfortunately I have to get back.'

'Oh, that's a shame,' the other woman sympathised. 'Particularly as it looks like being a nice day. I hope you'll stay with us again some time.'

Cory made herself smile. 'Some time—perhaps.'

But she knew in her heart she could never come back. That it would be too painful to relive, even at a distance, the crazy beauty of this night, with its tenderness and its savagery.

Now she had to go away, and try to forget.

The journey back was a nightmare. Because it was Sunday, there were engineering works taking place, and the train crawled along in between long pauses in the middle of nowhere.

It was mid-afternoon before she arrived back in London, and took a cab to her flat.

She would change, she thought, and do some food-shopping. Or perhaps even book a table at the neighbourhood French bistro, because it might be better to be with other people.

She paid off the cab and turned towards her door. And stopped, a sudden prickle of awareness edging into her consciousness.

She turned nervously, and saw him walking up the street towards her.

For a moment they stood facing each other. Cory bit her lip, expecting anger—recriminations.

But all he said, quite gently, was, 'Why did you run away?'

'Perhaps because I hate saying goodbye.'

'Then don't say it. Unlock your door and invite me in, and listen to what I have to say.'

'There's no need to say anything.' Bravely Cory lifted her chin. She thought, Don't apologise. Oh, please don't tell me you're sorry, because that I couldn't bear. 'It happened,' she went on, 'and it was wonderful, and now it's over. And we both get on with our own lives.'

Rome shook his head. 'It's not that simple, Cory.'

'If you're still thinking there might be a baby, it's my problem and I'll deal with it.' She gave him a travesty of her usual smile. 'There'll be no paternity suit. I won't ask you for anything.'

'I wasn't thinking that,' he said slowly. 'Of all the many thoughts I had on that hellish, lonely drive back, the prospect of becoming a father didn't even feature. Not that I'm against it in principle,' he added. 'But I feel it would be better for us to have some time just with each other before starting a family.'

She stared at him, her eyes enormous. She said, 'I think one of us must be going mad. What are you talking about?'

He sighed. 'I hadn't planned on doing this in the street,' he said, 'but I'm asking you to marry me, Cory. To be my wife. Will you?'

CHAPTER TEN

SHE said, 'I still can't believe this is happening. We—we've only just met...'

Rome pulled her further into his arms. 'If we're strangers,' he murmured. 'I don't think I'd survive being a close friend.'

They'd almost fallen into the flat on a wave of joy and laughter that had turned in seconds into a passion that would not be denied. He'd lifted her into his arms and carried her into the bedroom, mouths clinging, hands already beginning to tear at zips and buttons.

Now they lay sated and relaxed in each other's arms.

'Anyway,' he added softly, 'I think that in some way we've always known each other. Always been waiting to meet.'

She sighed. 'Then I'm glad I went to that charity ball. I didn't want to, you know.'

'Nor did I.' There was an odd note in his voice.

'And then we kept bumping into each other.' Cory giggled. 'Quite literally at times. I should have known it was fate.'

Rome was silent for a moment. Then he said, 'Cory, can I ask you to do something for me? Something a little strange which I can't explain just now.'

'How mysterious you sound.' She planted a row of tiny kisses on his throat. 'What is it?'

He hesitated again. 'I don't want you to tell anyone about us—at least not for a while.'

Cory looked up at him, her eyes wide with bewilderment.

'You mean—not even Gramps? But he'll be so happy for us, Rome. It's been his dearest wish for me to meet someone and fall in love. And I want the two men in my life to like each other. It's important to me.'

He said, 'It matters to me, too. But I have my reasons, even if I can't tell you what they are.' He grimaced slightly. 'And your grandfather may not be as delighted as you think. I'm no great catch for his only granddaughter.'

Cory was silent for a moment. 'Gramps is quite old-fashioned,' she said at last. 'I think he'd like it if you formally asked his permission.'

'I plan to,' he said. 'But we have to wait for a little while. Will you do that for me?'

'Yes,' she said. 'You know I will.' She gave a wondering laugh. 'Love at first sight, and now a secret engagement. This is all a dream, and soon I'm going to wake up. I know I am.'

'Don't say that, Cory.' His voice was suddenly harsh. 'Don't even think it.'

She looked up at him in surprise. 'Rome—are you all right?'

'Yes.' He kissed her, his mouth tender on hers. 'For the first time in my life, I believe I am.'

'And you really can't share this mystery with me?'

'Soon,' he said. 'I promise. I have some things to sort out first.'

'But I might be able to help.'

'I'm afraid you can't, *mia cara*.' His voice was regretful. 'Not this time.'

Her answering smile was faintly troubled. 'I understand.'

Only, she wasn't sure that she did. Only an hour ago she'd stood on the pavement, locked in Rome's arms, oblivious to everything but the joy opening inside her like a flower. The certainty that this was where she belonged.

She wanted to shout her happiness from the rooftops. But she couldn't. In fact, she couldn't tell a single soul. And she didn't know why.

She was aware that Shelley would say instantly that this was one mystery too many, and demand an immediate explanation before committing herself. That this was the reasonable—the rational course.

But I love him, she thought. And somehow reason and rationality don't seem so important any more.

There were so many things she wanted to ask him, so many gaps in her knowledge, but she supposed she would just have to be patient—and trust him.

He began to kiss her again, his fingers warm and arousing on her breast, and all doubts and vague uncertainties slid away as she turned to him, rapturous and yielding.

Later they had dinner at the bistro, and then watched an old film on television.

Cory had taken it for granted that Rome would be spending the night with her, but to her disappointment he told her he was going back to his own flat.

'I'm going away on business for a day or two,' he said. 'I need to pack and make an early start.'

'Must you go?' She couldn't disguise the sudden desolation in her voice.

He pulled her closer. 'The sooner I go, the sooner I'll be back,' he reminded her.

'I suppose so,' She paused. 'What's your flat like?'

She was hoping he'd say, Come back with me, and help me pack.

Instead, he shrugged. 'Dull—impersonal. Rather like a hotel room. You'd hate it.'

'I've nothing against hotel rooms.' Cory sent him a mischievous look. 'On the contrary. But if you really dislike it, you don't have to stay there.' She paused. 'You could always move in here.'

'Except that would blow our secret to smithereens,' Rome said drily. 'Besides, if you find out too soon that I snore and leave my clothes all over the floor, you might change your mind about marrying me. It's wiser to stay as we are.'

'Who cares about wisdom?'

'I think it's time one of us did,' he said wryly. 'We haven't been very sensible so far.'

'And now you're walking out on me.' She made it jokey, to hide the little pang of hurt. 'And I can't even comfort myself by talking about you.'

He framed her face in his hands, looking at her with heart-stopping tenderness. 'When we're married,' he said, 'you won't be able to get rid of me, and that's a guarantee.'

'I know I'm being really stupid.' She sighed. 'But I don't want to lose you. It's just too soon. I need to have you all to myself for a while.'

'You're not losing me,' Rome said steadily, 'because I'm taking you with me—in my heart, my mind and my soul. And when I come back you'll have the rest of my life—if you want it.'

She pulled him down to her. 'You think there's some doubt?' she whispered against his lips.

Yes, Rome thought, as he let himself into his flat. There was a chasm—an abyss of doubt.

More than once over the past forty-eight hours he'd come within a hair's breadth of telling her everything.

And perhaps, in the end, that was the only way to cut himself out of this maze of deceit he was enmeshed in.

Which, of course, he should have done before he asked her to marry him. He was a fool and more than a fool for that, he thought bitterly, but he hadn't been able to help himself—if that was any excuse.

Her enraptured response to his loving had sent him over the edge into a kind of madness where nothing mattered other than she should belong to him for ever.

And then he'd woken and found her gone.

He'd argued with himself every mile of that headlong drive back from Suffolk, trying to convince himself that she'd done the right thing. That the enmity between their two families was too strong, and there was no way they'd ever be allowed to be together.

Her affection for her grandfather shone out of her. How would she react when she found that he, Rome, was being paid to seduce her with the aim of extorting more money from Arnold Grant? She'd think that every bad thing she'd heard about the Sansoms was fully justified. He'd about been able to see the stricken look in the clear eyes as she turned away from him.

But he hadn't allowed himself to think like that, or he might really have gone mad. His priority—his pressing, urgent need—had been to find her—to talk to her about some of the feelings that were tearing him apart. And to ask her to wait for him while he sorted out the stinking mess his life had become.

But when he'd seen her, standing in front of him, he'd lost his last precarious hold on reality and asked her to marry him instead.

He'd had no right to do anything of the kind, and he knew it. But there was no way he wished the words unsaid.

And now he had to fight to keep her, along with Montedoro. And with no real idea even how to begin, he thought with bitter weariness.

The light on his answer-machine was blinking, and when

he pressed the 'play' button, he got Matt's angry voice, demanding to know where he was.

It was a good thing that he hadn't yielded to the overwhelming temptation to bring Cory back here with him, Rome thought, his mouth twisting wryly as he listened. Because Matt Sansom on the rampage defied explanation.

'You'd better have some good news for me when I call next time,' his grandfather rumbled furiously at the end of his tirade. 'Because I've had enough of this.'

'Which makes two of us,' Rome muttered, and deleted the message.

'You seem very pleased with yourself these days.' Arnold Grant directed a shrewd glance at Cory, who was singing softly to herself as she sat in front of the computer screen.

'I do?' Cory realised she was blushing. 'I—I can't think why,' she hedged.

Arnold glanced over her shoulder. 'Been making a killing on the market?' He sounded amused. 'Since when have you been interested in stocks and shares?'

'For quite a while.' She gave him a sedate smile. 'It's my hobby.'

'You're full of surprises, child. You look different, too.' He gave her a long look. 'What have you done to your hair?'

Cory put up a self-conscious hand. 'Just a few highlights.' She paused. 'You don't approve?'

Arnold said drily, 'I don't think it's my approval you're looking for.' He paused. 'So, who is he?'

Cory studied the screen with extra concentration. 'I don't know what you mean.'

'In other words, I'm to mind my own business.' Arnold nodded. 'But ultimately, my girl, your happiness and well-being are my business. Remember that, please.' He paused.

'So why haven't you mentioned him before? Is he someone I wouldn't approve of?'

Cory bit her lip, wishing with all her heart that she hadn't pledged to keep her relationship with Rome a secret. Especially when it was impossible to hide the sheen on her hair, the colour in her cheeks, the swing in her step—all the tell-tale signs of happiness.

And this might have been the perfect moment to enlist her grandfather's support.

'No. And I haven't told you about him because I haven't known him that long, and it's too soon for formal introductions. Besides, he's away at the moment on business,' she added quickly.

'Hmm.' Arnold was silent for a moment. Then he said gruffly, 'Is it serious?'

She said a quiet, 'Yes—I hope so,' and was frankly relieved when he did not ask her to elaborate further.

Rome had called once, leaving an outrageous message on her answering machine which had made her blush to her toes, but giving no clue as to when he would be back.

This was the third day and night, she thought forlornly, and it felt like for ever.

For the rest of the afternoon she was aware of her grandfather's speculative gaze, and was quite glad when he told her that she could leave early. A certain abruptness in his tone told her that he was hurt because she hadn't confided in him more fully.

Up to now, she thought ruefully, her life had been pretty much an open book where he was concerned—and fairly dull reading at that.

But what would his reaction be when he found she was planning to live in Italy?

I'm all he has, she thought, troubled, as she made her

way home. But I'll just have to cross that bridge when I come to it.

Earlier that day, Rome had been on his way back from the North of England, where he'd been following up a list of contacts that Allessandro had given him. And a gratifying number, it seemed, were ready to give the Montedoro vintages a trial.

At any other time Rome would have been well-satisfied. He might even have been turning cartwheels.

But he could not escape from the knowledge that the wine he was selling might soon no longer belong to him.

But if he could demonstrate that his business was prospering, surely he'd be able to attract some independent financial backing somewhere, to ensure that he and Cory would have a life together at Montedoro?

However, nothing was certain in this uncertain world, he reminded himself bitterly, and there were powerful forces stacked against him.

But, as Steve had once told him, if you didn't stake everything, you didn't deserve to win. And he was fighting for his future. And for Cory.

When he got back to his flat, he found several messages from Matt Sansom, angrily bidding him to pick up the phone.

But what he had to say to his grandfather needed to be delivered in person, he thought without pleasure.

Even when the sun was shining Matt's house looked grotesque, he thought, as he parked his car and walked up to the door.

Today, it was answered by a woman in a neat overall. He asked for Miss Sansom, and was conducted through the house to a large elaborate conservatory at the rear. Here, among a welter of large and faintly menacing green plants, he found Kit Sansom, tranquilly engaged with some *petit point*.

She laid it aside when she saw him. 'Rome, my dear.' She held out a hand. 'I didn't know you were coming. Father didn't mention it.'

'He doesn't know.' He sat down on one of the cushioned wicker chairs she indicated. 'I suppose you know why he sent for me originally—what he wanted me to do?'

'Oh, yes.' She sighed sadly. 'He's quite obsessed, you know. Although, to be fair, they both are.'

Rome leaned forward. 'How did it start, Aunt Kit?' he asked quietly. 'Have you any idea?'

'Oh, yes.' Her voice was matter-of-fact. 'I knew a long time ago—even before Sarah left. My godmother told me everything.'

'Can you tell me?'

Kit Sansom folded her hands in her lap, her expression reflective. 'To begin with it was just business rivalry—even healthy competition—although there probably wasn't much love lost between them even then.

'But in those days your grandfather had other things on his mind as well, not just making money. He'd fallen passionately in love, and become engaged to this lovely girl. He was planning his wedding—his life with her.

'He had to go away for a few days on business, and while he was gone his fiancée went to a friend's birthday party. Where she was introduced to Arnold Grant.'

She smiled sadly. 'Apparently, it was the kind of encounter you only read about—the genuine *coup de foudre*. Once they'd met, nothing else existed for either of them. So she broke off her engagement to your grandfather and married Arnold Grant instead.

'My godmother said Matt was like a crazy man. That he went round vowing all kinds of revenge on them both, but everyone assumed that he'd get over it in time and be reasonable. Only, he never did.'

She sighed again. 'From that moment on, Arnold Grant was his sworn enemy. At first he wouldn't retaliate, no matter what your grandfather did, but eventually, inevitably, Matt went too far, and it became mutual—a full-scale feud with no holds barred.'

'*Dio*—it's unbelievable,' Rome said. 'To go on bearing a grudge like that—hating for all these years. Filling the house with it. No wonder my mother ran away.' He paused. 'Why didn't it stop when he met my grandmother—found someone else to love?'

Kit shook her head. 'My father married my mother because he needed a wife, and she was available.' She spoke without rancour. 'The problem was he wanted someone to play hostess when he entertained clients, and Mother was basically shy, and rather timid. I take after her, I think. Also, he wanted a son to inherit his business empire, as Arnold had, and she gave him two daughters.

'I think she loved him,' she added quietly. 'But she couldn't compete with the ghost of the woman he'd loved and lost—Elizabeth Cory. Sarah and I were always aware of—tensions between them. This was never a happy house.'

Rome drew a sharp breath. 'If he loved Elizabeth so much, how could he contemplate destroying her granddaughter?' he demanded roughly. 'Using her as a weapon in this senseless vendetta?'

'To hurt as he was hurt, perhaps.' Her voice was grave. 'It's all so dark and twisted that it's difficult to know. Sarah was lucky to escape—to find some happiness.'

He looked at her. 'Were you never tempted to leave—and not come back?'

'Oh, yes.' She smiled a little. 'So very often. But then

he'd have had no one, and somehow I just couldn't do it.'
She returned his gaze. 'What are you going to do, Rome?'

'I'm going to try and stop it,' he said. 'Because it's gone
on too long. And I won't allow it to damage me—or the
girl I love. Because I'm going to marry Elizabeth's granddaughter, Aunt Kit.'

'Ah, Rome.' Her voice was tired. 'Do you really think
they'll let you?'

He smiled at her. 'I grew up with a gambling man, Aunt
Kit. I just have to take that chance.'

There were sudden tears in her eyes. She said, 'Rome—
be careful. Be very careful.' She paused, looking down at
her hands. 'Was he good to her—the gambling man? Did
he make my little sister happy? Please tell me he did.'

Rome said gently, 'Yes, he adored her. He was kind,
laid-back and humorous, and we both thought the world of
him.'

'I'm so glad,' she said. 'Glad that she found someone to
love her. She hadn't had much luck up to then—either with
her father or yours.'

Rome was very still. He said, 'Aunt Kit—are you saying
you know who my father was?'

'Oh, yes,' she said calmly. 'She needed to confide in
someone—but I'd guessed long before. Guessed—and
feared for her.'

'Will you tell me?'

'If it's really what you want.' She saw him nod, and
sighed faintly. 'His name was James Farrar, and he was a
business associate of your grandfather. Dark and handsome,
but considerably older than she was. I sometimes wondered
if that was the attraction. If she was really looking for another father figure. Someone who wasn't eaten up by his
need for revenge. She knew he was married, but he told
her he was getting divorced.'

'And she believed him?' Rome asked bitterly. 'My God.'

'You mustn't blame her, my dear.' Her voice was kind. 'Up to that time she'd led a pretty sheltered life—we both had. When Sarah told him she was pregnant, he went completely to pieces. Begged her not to tell Matt, or he'd be ruined. Said all the money was his wife's, and she'd throw him out. Offered to pay for an abortion.

'She told him to go, and never saw him again. But she wouldn't identify him to Matt.' She sighed. 'He stormed at her—called her terrible names—but she was like a rock.

'He tried to make her have an abortion, too, but she refused. She told me that she might have messed up her life, but some good was going to come out of it. All the same, she wasn't going to bring her child into a house of hate either—so she ran away.'

There was a silence, the Rome said, 'What became of—him?'

'He died about ten years ago. A car accident. He'd started to drink heavily.' She put a hand on his arm. 'I wish it was a nicer story.'

'I can see why she wouldn't want to remember him.' Rome's face was sombre.

'But she was happy in the end.' His aunt paused. 'I've kept her secret a long time,' she said quietly. 'I hope you'll continue to respect that.'

'I'll tell Cory one day,' Rome said. 'But only her. And—thank you.' He got to his feet. 'Now I'd better go and talk to my grandfather.'

'You've asked her to marry you, and she's agreed?' Matt Sansom released a shout of astonished laughter. 'Well, that's fast work by anyone's standards. You've lived up to my expectations, boy, and more.'

He was dressed today, and sitting in a high-backed chair

by his bedroom window, a rug over his knees, his face alive
with malice.

Rome said coldly, 'I hope that's not a compliment, because that's not all of it. The marriage will be for real.
When I return to Italy Cory's going with me, as my wife.'

Matt was suddenly very still. The calm, Rome thought,
before the storm. But when he spoke his voice was mild.

'You're saying you've fallen in love with her—with the
Ice Maiden? How did this come about?'

I have you to thank,' Rome said. 'After all, you brought
us together.'

'So I did,' Matt said softly. 'So I did.'

'And she's Elizabeth Cory's granddaughter,' Rome
added. 'Things may not be as hopeless for me as you believe. I intend to fight you for Montedoro.'

Matt stared at him. 'If you're hoping that Arnold Grant
will give you his blessing, and a handsome settlement, then
you're an even bigger fool than I took you for.'

'I'm going to try and persuade him to listen to reason,'
Rome returned levelly. 'To tell him what I've told you.
That the feud must end. That it's too costly, and too dam-
aging in all kinds of ways.'

'And you think he'll listen?' Matt laughed again,
hoarsely. 'I wish you luck.' He paused. 'Have you said all
you came to say?'

'Yes.'

'Then you can go, and be damned to you. I need to
think.'

Rome nodded, and rose to his feet.

At the door, Rome paused. He said, 'I wish you'd meet
Cory—to get to know her. I think it would make a difference.'

'Yes,' Matt said, almost absently. 'Yes, it might. I'll
think about that, too. Yes, I'll certainly think about that…'

As Rome reached the foot of the stairs, he heard his name called softly and saw his aunt beckoning to him from the drawing room.

'How did it go?' She closed the door quietly.

Rome shrugged. 'Not well,' he said. 'But he's going to think it over. Maybe it's a first step.'

'Yes,' Kit Sansom said drily. 'But in which direction? However, that's not what I want to talk about.' She picked up a small jeweller's box from a side table, and handed it to him. 'I'd like to offer you this. My mother gave it to me before she died, and I'm sure she'd wish you to have it.'

Rome opened the box and saw a ring, a large amethyst surrounded by small pearls in an antique setting.

He said slowly, 'It's quite beautiful, Aunt Kit, but I can't accept it. It belongs to you.'

She smiled at him. 'My dear, I've never worn it. My hands are the wrong shape. And I don't remember my mother wearing it either,' she added thoughtfully. 'She always said that amethysts weren't her favourite stone. Anyway, I'd like to know it was being put to a proper use at last. It's far too lovely to spend its life in a box. Give it to your Cory—please.'

Rome put his hands on her shoulders and kissed her cheek.

He said, gently, 'I want you to be our first visitor at Montedoro.'

She patted his arm. 'I'd love it. But first you have to win your battle.' Her voice was sober suddenly, almost fearful. 'And, Rome, I say again—do take great care. You may not know what you're up against.'

CHAPTER ELEVEN

CORY let herself into her flat, hung away her trenchcoat, filled the kettle and set it to boil, then kicked off her shoes.

All set, she thought wryly, for another quiet evening at home. But she didn't feel tranquil. She was restless—on edge—prowling round the living room with her mug of tea, glancing through the television listings and finding nothing to interest her, picking up a magazine and tossing it down again, loading her CD player and switching it off halfway through a track.

She switched on her computer, checked the latest share prices, then abandoned that, too.

She supposed she could make a start on her evening meal, but none of the food in the fridge held any great appeal either.

She rang Shelley and left a call-back message on her machine, although it was likely that her friend, who'd had three young men circling round her at the last count, had gone straight out to dinner from work.

She was just reaching for the phone to dial a take-away service when it rang.

She grabbed the receiver, 'Hi...'

Rome said softly, 'Open your door.'

She uttered a shriek, dropped the phone, and leapt for the door, flinging herself into his arms. 'You're back— you're here...'

'I'm also deafened.' Rome pulled her close, kissing her mouth hungrily. *'Dio,'* he muttered when he raised his head at last, 'I've missed you so.'

'Not as much as I've missed you.' She clung to him shamelessly, arms round his neck, legs round his waist.

Rome reached down with difficulty to retrieve a bouquet of long-stemmed crimson roses propped against the wall, and carried Cory and the flowers into the flat, kicking the door shut behind them.

He put her down on the sofa and handed her the flowers. 'For you, *mia cara*.'

'They're wonderful.' Cory luxuriously inhaled the rich dark scent. 'I'd better put them in water.'

Rome took them from her hands. 'I think they can survive for a little while without attention.' He tossed them on to the table, then sank down beside her, pulling off his coat. 'I, on the other hand, cannot,' he added huskily.

Her hands were shaking as they unbuttoned his shirt. She pushed it from his shoulders, then dragged her shell-pink sweater over her head and fumbled to release herself from the folds of her matching wool skirt.

Rome, too, was hastily stripping off his clothes, his eyes fixed on her as if he was afraid she might suddenly vanish.

He threw cushions down on to the floor and drew her down to him, his hands rediscovering her feverishly, his mouth drinking her—draining her—until at last he lifted her over him, his eyes smiling up into hers, to join her body to his.

She took him slowly, her breath escaping in a low, sweet moan as she felt his hardness filling her ever more deeply.

His hands reached up to cup her breasts, his thumbs lightly brushing her nipples as she began to move on him, her eyes half-closed and her head thrown back, exposing the taut, delicate line of her throat.

In a silence disturbed only by their panting breath they established a rhythm—found a harmony together as their bodies rose and fell.

Rome caressed her with words as well as his hands, his eyes darkening sensually as he watched her enraptured face.

He let his hands stray down her backbone, moulding the swell of her buttocks and trailing over her flanks.

He stroked her ribcage and shaped her slim waist, his hands trailing a delicious path over the concavity of her stomach down to the silky triangle between her thighs.

A sob broke from her as his fingers began to tease her with intimate subtlety, moving softly, fluttering on her.

She felt her control slipping as, deep inside, she sensed the first stirrings of pleasure.

And heard him whisper, 'No, *mia cara*—not yet.'

Again and again he brought her to the edge of extinction, then retreated.

And she rode him wildly, her body slicked with sweat, her voice a soundless scream, begging for release.

When it came, it was explosive, and she cried out harshly as her body achieved its fierce freedom. Within seconds Rome had followed her, groaning his delight as his body shook with the force of his climax.

Then they collapsed, breathless, boneless, into each other's arms.

Eventually he said, with a ghost of laughter in his voice, 'Perhaps you really did miss me.'

'I kept thinking that you might never come back—that I'd never see you again.' She couldn't dissemble, pretend prudent indifference. 'Not any more.'

'I have something for you.'

'I know.' She stretched like a contented cat. 'My beautiful roses.'

He reached for his coat. 'No, more than that.' He extracted the little square box and handed it to her.

Cory gasped out loud as she saw the deep mauve of the amethyst, surrounded by creamy pearls.

She said huskily, 'It's—wonderful. And it's my birth-stone, too. How did you know?'

'I didn't,' he admitted ruefully. 'It's a family ring, so this makes you my family for evermore.'

He took her left hand and kissed it, then slid the ring over the knuckle of her third finger. It fitted perfectly.

Her voice shook a little. 'Does this mean we're officially engaged?'

'Almost.' He kissed her gently. 'I still have to get your grandfather's blessing, so it might be better to wait for that. Until then you could always wear it on your other hand, in public anyway.'

'I'd even wear it through my nose.' Cory's smile lit up the world. 'Just as long as I don't have to hide it away in its box.'

They spent the evening doing small, mundane things, content to be sharing them with each other. Cory put her roses in water and cooked some pasta, while Rome made a rich aromatic sauce out of tomatoes, bacon, herbs and garlic.

Afterwards, they went to bed, and slept wrapped in each other's arms.

And, for once, Cory forgot to set her alarm for the morning.

When she eventually opened her eyes, she yelped with dismay.

She was going to be late for work and, granddaughter or no, Arnold was a stickler for punctuality in the mornings.

Rome's arms scooped her back. 'You're running away again,' he muttered sleepily.

'Only to work.'

'Call in sick.'

'I can't.' She wriggled free. 'You want Gramps to like you, don't you?'

'I want you to like me.'

'I will—I do. This evening I'll think the world of you, I swear.' She scrambled out of bed. 'But now I have to rush.'

Even so, she wasn't surprised when he joined her in the shower.

'You shouldn't be here.' Her breathing fragmented as he began to soap her, his hands lingering on her breasts and thighs. 'Oh, God—I don't—I really don't have—time—for this…'

Rome kissed her wet shoulder. 'Really and truly?'

'Cross my heart.' Her pulses were going mad, and her knees were weak, but she spoke with determination and he laughed.

'Then I'll be good, and make you some coffee instead.'

Cory was standing in her robe, drying her hair, when the door buzzer sounded.

'Shall I get it?' Rome called from the kitchen.

'I'd better,' she said. 'It might be the postman, early for once.' And, 'All right, I'm coming,' she called, as the buzzer made another imperative summons.

She went barefoot to the door, pulling the robe more closely round her and tightening its sash.

She'd planned to say, 'I hope this is a seriously interesting parcel.' But all words died on her lips when she opened the door and saw who was confronting her.

'And about time, too,' Sonia said tartly. 'Well, don't just stand there. Ask me in. It's freezing out here.'

'Mother,' Cory said, dry-mouthed, as she spotted a small mountain of luggage piled up in the passage. 'What are you doing here?'

'I was in New York, seeing friends,' Sonia said lightly. 'And I decided to extend my trip and check on my only daughter.' She leaned forward, air-kissing Cory on both cheeks. 'So, I caught the red-eye and here I am.'

Well, there was no denying that, Cory thought ruefully, assimilating the pale blonde hair, artfully coiffed, the immaculate maquillage, the close fitting dove-coloured trouser suit that showed off her mother's slim, toned figure to the best advantage, and the fur jacket draped casually round her shoulders.

As usual, Sonia made her feel as if she'd been swapped at birth.

She swept past Cory into the flat, and looked around her. 'My God, what a small apartment. How many bedrooms do you have?'

'Just the one,' Cory admitted.

Sonia raised her eyes to heaven. 'In that case, painful as it will be for both of us, I'll be staying with your grandfather. Is that coffee I smell?'

Cory felt hollow. 'Yes.'

Sonia made for the kitchen, then stopped abruptly, with a gasp that owed more to genuine surprise than her usual talent for drama.

'And just who are you?' she demanded sharply.

Rome continued to pour black coffee into beakers. 'My name's Rome d'Angelo, *signora*. And I'm seeing your daughter.'

'And she, in turn, is seeing you.' Sonia's voice held a distinct edge. 'About ninety per cent of you, or even a hundred, if that towel slips any further.'

'I'll make sure it doesn't—at least in your presence.' Unperturbed, Rome handed her a beaker.

'Thank you.' Sonia tasted the brew suspiciously, then nodded. 'You make good coffee. Just one of your many talents, I'm sure,' she added waspishly.

'The least of them,' Rome confirmed, unfazed. 'And another is to spot when I'm in the way. I'm sure you both have so much to catch up on, so I'll clear out and leave you to it.'

Cory followed him to the bedroom. 'Will I see you tonight?' she asked unhappily.

He hesitated. 'You may have other obligations. I'll call you.' He dropped the towel to the floor and began, swiftly, to dress. 'I take it this visit was unexpected?'

'A bolt from the blue. My mother,' Cory said with some bitterness, 'is a creature of impulse.'

He slanted an amused look at her. 'Perhaps that's something you have in common.'

Cory gave him a troubled look. 'You realise the cat's well and truly out of the bag? Sonia doesn't have a discreet bone in her body.'

'Yes,' Rome said with a certain grimness, 'I realise, and I'm going to deal with it.' He wrapped his arms round her and kissed her hard, making her senses spin.

'Don't let her get to you, *cara*,' he whispered. 'And I'll see you later.'

As she picked up her ring from the night table and slid it on to her right hand, Cory could hear him bidding Sonia a courteous goodbye.

Steeling herself, she rejoined her mother in the living room.

'My, my, aren't you the dark horse?' Seated on the sofa, legs crossed, Sonia gave her daughter a searching look. 'And just when I thought you'd settled for being an old maid.'

Cory shrugged. 'I discovered I didn't have to settle for anything,' she returned stiffly.

'Hmm.' Sonia studied her frowningly, taking account of her flushed cheeks and reddened mouth. 'What does he call himself—Rome? What kind of name is that?'

Cory lifted her chin. 'His.'

'I see.' Sonia sounded amused. 'Well, don't be so protective, darling. I'm sure your Rome d'Angelo can look after himself, and has been doing so for some years, if I'm any judge.' She paused. 'D'Angelo,' she repeated thoughtfully. 'You know, that rings a bell. Someone I once met in Miami...'

Cory shook her head. 'Rome lives in Italy. He has a vineyard there.'

'How very romantic,' Sonia said. 'And I know it wasn't him that I met. I think I'd have remembered such a—spectacular young man.' She drank some coffee. 'Where did you meet him?'

'At a charity ball, originally. And then we discovered we were neighbours—almost. And it went from there.'

'You can say that again.' Sonia's voice was dry. 'Well, how very convenient, and such a coincidence, too.' She paused. 'And what does Arnold think of him?'

Cory hesitated. 'They haven't met—yet.'

'Is that your choice—or the boyfriend's?'

'Mine,' Cory said shortly. 'And isn't it a little late for *you* to start being protective?'

Sonia looked at her consideringly, then shrugged. 'Maybe you have a point.' She looked at Cory's hand. 'What a beautiful ring. Where did you get it?'

'It was a present,' Cory said quietly. 'From Rome.'

'A love token,' Sonia said brightly. 'How very sweet.' She became brisk again. 'Call me a cab, will you, honey? I'm going over to Arnold's now, before these tiny rooms give me claustrophobia.'

'Give me five minutes to get dressed, and I'll come with you,' Cory offered.

Sonia shuddered. 'I wish you wouldn't talk about getting dressed in five minutes,' she said peevishly. 'I suggest you start paying a little more attention to your appearance—

especially if you want to hang on to a piece of work like Mr d'Angelo. I never let your father see me in the mornings until I'd combed my hair and put on my mascara.'

'I doubt if I'll have time for such niceties,' Cory said lightly. 'Not on a vineyard in Tuscany.'

'Well, you're not there yet,' Sonia said sharply. 'But there's no need for you to come to Arnold's right away. It's going to be quite a reunion after all this time, and we'll have plenty to talk over. So, why don't you take it easy?'

'One of the preferred topics of conversation being myself, no doubt?' Cory's tone was cutting.

Sonia sighed. 'Honey,' she said, 'I may not have made a big success of the role, but I'm still your mother, and, believe it or not, I'm concerned for you. And so is your grandfather—sure you'll be a topic. A major one. So why don't you let us have our discussion, and meet us for lunch at twelve-thirty? We should be all done by then.' She glanced at her watch, and winced. 'My God, this time difference is a killer.'

When she eventually left, in a haze of perfume, Cory sank down on the sofa, curling her legs under her in an unconsciously defensive posture.

Sonia's arrival was a totally unforeseen complication, she thought unhappily. And one she could well have done without.

She'd always known that it wouldn't be easy convincing Gramps that she'd finally met the man she wanted to spend the rest of her life with—especially when she'd known Rome such a short time. Although he of all people should understand, she thought with a sigh. Only it didn't always work out like that.

Still, she'd been sure that she could talk him round. But if he was aligned with her mother...

She shook her head. That was a pretty formidable combination.

Sonia had made it clear she had misgivings about Rome—echoing all Cory's own early doubts, if she was honest.

Why, indeed, should a man like that choose a girl like her?

'Because he loves me,' she said aloud, lifting her head in affirmation. 'Because we love each other.'

But some of the radiance of last night had faded, and, do what she would, she could not summon it back.

She looked down at the amethyst, glowing on her hand. My talisman, she told herself. And raised it to her lips.

Over in Chelsea, Sonia wasted no time.

'When I got to Cory's apartment today there was a man there,' she said, after the usual greetings and enquiries had been exchanged, and her luggage taken upstairs to the guest suite.

Arnold looked down his nose. 'Suddenly turned prude, my dear? This is the twenty-first century.'

Sonia snorted. 'No, of course I haven't. But how much do you know about this guy?'

'Very little,' Arnold admitted, frowning. 'She's being rather secretive about him.'

'I don't blame her,' Sonia returned. 'If he belonged to me, I'd find a deserted house in a deep forest and chain him to the bed.' She paused. 'He calls himself Rome d'Angelo.'

Arnold thought, then shook his head. 'I haven't heard of him.'

'Then I feel you should make his acquaintance without delay.' Sonia pursed her lips. 'She's wearing a ring.'

'An engagement ring?' He was clearly startled.

'Wrong hand, but what do I know?' Sonia frowned. 'It's a lovely thing—looks antique and expensive—a big amethyst with pearls around it.' She sighed. 'Pearls for tears, they say, but maybe Cory's not superstitious.'

'An amethyst?' Arnold's tone sharpened. 'Are you sure?'

'Those are the mauve stones, aren't they? Why do you ask?'

There was an odd silence, then he said, 'It just seems a strange choice for an engagement ring—if that's what it is. Diamonds are more conventional.'

Sonia leaned back in her chair. 'I don't think,' she said slowly, 'that convention means a great deal to the sexy Mr d'Angelo. I feel we should start making a few discreet enquiries about him.'

Arnold was staring into the distance, eyes narrowed and mouth set grimly.

Lunch in Chelsea was a strained affair. Arnold was silent and preoccupied, and Sonia laughed and talked a little too much.

It was like a dream she'd once had, Cory thought, pushing poached salmon round her plate. She'd found herself on stage with the curtain about to go up—and she was wearing the wrong costume and knew none of her lines.

When coffee was served, Sonia rose from the table, announcing she was off to get a massage and beauty treatment—'Best way to cope with jet lag, honey'—and Cory found herself alone with her grandfather.

There was a silence between them that Cory, for the first time in her life, felt unable to break. She knew that she had to sit and wait for him to speak.

Eventually, he said, 'This man you're seeing—I asked yesterday if you were serious about him. You didn't see fit to mention you were living with him. Why?'

Cory lifted her chin. 'Because we're not actually living together.'

'Ah,' he said. 'You just allow him to use you when the mood takes him. Is that it?'

She stared at him, shocked. 'Gramps—don't. You make it sound so sordid.'

'Perhaps I find it so, Cory. Knowing that my only granddaughter is sharing her body with a man she's apparently known for days, hours and minutes, rather than weeks, months, years.'

She said steadily, 'It's not really such a new thing. We fell in love, just as you did when you first saw Gran. If it had happened now, instead of years ago, you'd be doing the same thing.'

'Don't dare to compare the situations.' His voice was harsh. 'In my day you offered a woman security and respect along with passion.'

He paused. 'What do you really know about this man? Your mother says she now remembers meeting a Steve d'Angelo in Florida some years ago. He was a gambler, a man who lived by his wits and made a living by calculating the weaknesses of others. Are they related?'

'His stepfather.'

'And his real father?'

Cory bit her lip. 'He never knew him.'

'I see,' Arnold said coldly. He looked at her hand. 'I understand he gave you that ring. It's a very unusual design—very distinctive. Do you know how he came by it?'

Cory got to her feet, her face very white. She said, 'Just what are you implying? That Rome stole it?'

'Or won it at cards, perhaps.' There was an odd urgency in his tone.

'Then you're wrong. It's a family ring,' she said huskily. 'Does that satisfy you?'

'A family ring,' he repeated slowly. 'But from which member of the family, I wonder?'

'Does it matter?' Cory shook her head. 'I can't believe I'm taking part in this—interrogation. You've always claimed you wanted me to fall in love. I didn't realise you intended to investigate my lover.'

'You seem to think I'm doing him an injustice.' Arnold seemed to rouse himself, looking at her with eyes that hardly seemed to see her. 'And perhaps I am. But, until we meet, I'm having to rely on hearsay. Maybe you should allow him to speak for himself.'

There was a silence, then she said, 'I love him, Grandfather. I can't live without him.'

'You think that now, child.' There was a note of appeal in his voice. 'But you'll probably fall in and out of love several times before you meet the right man for you.'

She said, 'Would you have got over Gran so easily—and gone on to someone else? I don't think so. And with Rome and I there's no one else involved either.'

There was a wild look in his eyes. 'You don't think so? How can you know?'

'Because I trust him—just as Gran trusted you. You knew she was the only one, and so did she. And I'm your granddaughter, so maybe it's in my genes.'

She went to the door. Turned. 'And please don't call me ''child'' again. I'm a woman now—Rome's woman.'

His glance was heavy. 'For good or ill?'

She said, 'Yes,' and went out, closing the door behind her.

Arnold Grant sat very still for a moment. Then, moving slowly and stiffly, he reached for the telephone.

CHAPTER TWELVE

'THIS,' Cory said passionately, 'has to rank as one of the worst days of my life.'

'Thanks,' Rome said drily. 'Shall I get dressed and leave?'

'I'm sorry.' She kissed him repentantly. 'I mean apart from the last couple of hours—which is evening anyway, so it doesn't count.'

I'm relieved to hear it. And I told you not to let your mother get to you, sweetheart. You should have listened.'

'Oh, it wasn't Ma,' Cory said bitterly. 'She cleared out to the beauty parlour and left me to the Spanish Inquisition.' She moved restlessly. 'It was awful. Gramps was like a stranger, staring me down, behaving as if I was on trial—or you were.'

'What did he say?' Rome asked curiously.

'Oh, nothing much. Just that you were a liar, and a con-man, and possibly a thief. Usual stuff.' She shook her head. 'In the end I slammed out of the house. I spent the afternoon in Hyde Park, just walking, trying to clear my head.'

Rome was silent for a moment. 'Darling, I think it's time your grandfather and I had a serious talk.'

'It seems he does, too,' Cory admitted reluctantly. 'When I got home there was a message on the machine. Apparently, he wants us to go to dinner tomorrow night.'

'Did you accept?'

'I haven't replied yet. He doesn't deserve it. Besides, I don't know if I can stand it. More questions over the soup.

Final arguments with the main course. Sentence of death pronounced during dessert.'

'I think we should go,' Rome told her. 'It could be an olive branch.'

Cory pulled a face. 'All the better to beat us with.'

'I really need to see him.' His voice was gentle. 'Get a few things straight.'

'Then I'll tell him yes.' She sighed. 'We didn't have our secret very long, did we?'

'It's not always good,' Rome said, his face suddenly brooding, 'to keep things from people you love. The longer it goes on, the harder they are to explain.'

'You sound very old and wise.' There was sudden laughter in her voice.

'I haven't been very wise at all,' he said. 'Not from the start of all this. As for being old…' The hand that had been curled round the curve of her hip moved without haste and to devastating effect. 'Let's see about that—shall we?'

'Yes,' she managed dry-mouthed. 'Oh, yes, Rome. *Rome…*'

She didn't go to work the following day, and Arnold did not ring to enquire where she was, so it seemed he was not expecting her.

In spite of the harsh words between them, Cory hated being on bad terms with him.

But after tonight, she told herself, everything will be fine.

She put on a new dress for the occasion, a silky jersey in a subtle aubergine shade. And she put her ring on her left hand.

Rome said, 'You look beautiful.'

He was smiling as he looked at her in the mirror, but his face was strained.

'And so do you.' She had never seen him in a formal dark suit before. 'Gramps will be swept off his feet.'

On their way out, she snapped off one of the crimson roses that was still in bud, and tucked it into his buttonhole.

He was on edge all the way to Chelsea, his hands gripping the wheel as if he was drowning.

Cory stole a troubled look at him. 'Rome—are you sure you want to go through with this—seeking his blessing?'

'I've never been so sure of anything.' His voice was husky. 'But, Cory—there's something I should tell you.'

She said, 'I hope this isn't the moment you reveal you're already married. Because Grandfather would not take that in good part. Other than that, we're home and dry.' She paused. 'We're also here.'

As she rang the bell, she said. 'So, what was it you wanted to tell me?'

He shook his head. 'I can't talk to you about it now. I think I should see your grandfather first.' He put his hands on her shoulders. His voice was serious. 'The only thing that matters, Cory, is that I love you. Never lose sight of that—please.'

'Well, it all seems relatively civilised,' she murmured as the housekeeper conducted them to the drawing room. 'No paid assassins lurking. After the way he was talking the other day, I did wonder.'

'He's quite right to be cautious,' Rome said soberly. 'But everything's going to be fine. You'll see.'

And it seemed they had indeed been worrying unnecessarily. When they entered the drawing room Arnold came to meet them, smiling affably as Cory performed the necessary introductions.

As they shook hands, the two men exchanged overtly measuring glances.

'My daughter-in-law I believe you've met,' Arnold said.

'Oh, yes.' Sonia was smiling from one of the sofas. She was elegant in black, with magnificent diamonds in her ears and on her wrists. 'We're quite old friends. I'm glad to see you dress for dinner if not for breakfast, Mr d'Angelo.'

'I haven't invited any other guests to meet you,' Arnold went on. 'I thought we'd have a quiet family party. Sherry?'

'Thank you.' Rome accepted with a smile, but he wasn't fooled. His sixth sense was warning him that the knives were out for him here in this luxurious room, with its wall sconces and brocaded furniture.

He said quietly, 'I hope I can have a private talk with you during the evening, Mr Grant.'

'Oh, there's no need for that,' Arnold said. 'We can say all that needs to be said here, in the open. Among friends.' He handed Rome his sherry. 'I take it there's something you want to ask me? Something of a personal nature?'

Rome's brows drew together sharply, but he kept his voice cool. 'Yes, there is, although I hadn't planned to do it in quite this way.'

'It was to be over the brandy and cigars, perhaps? When I was feeling mellow.' There was a faint smile playing round the older man's mouth. A smile that held neither humour nor warmth. 'Well, say what you came here to say, Mr d'Angelo. I'm listening.'

'Very well.' Rome spoke levelly. 'The truth is, Mr Grant, that Cory and I love each other. I've come to ask formally for your blessing to marry her.'

'The truth?' Arnold said meditatively. 'As in the whole truth—and nothing but the truth?' He shook his head. 'I don't think so.'

'Grandfather,' Cory protested angrily.

'Sit down, my dear.' His voice was marginally kinder. 'I'm afraid I have an unpleasant shock for you. You see, your suitor is not quite what he seems. I'm sure you already know that he's not Italian, but are you aware that d'Angelo isn't his real name—just the one he took from his stepfather?'

'Yes,' Cory said. 'Yes, I am.'

'But did he tell what he is really called—the name he was born to? I think not. Perhaps you'd like to enlighten us now—Mr d'Angelo.'

There was real venom in the older man's voice.

Groaning inwardly, Rome met his gaze, then turned to Cory, who was looking bewildered.

He said gently, 'It's Sansom, *mia cara*. My mother was Sarah Sansom, Matt's younger daughter.' He glanced at Arnold, his mouth hard. 'Is that what you wanted to hear?'

'Part of it.' Arnold nodded. 'And please believe this gives me no pleasure. My grandchild is very dear to me— as of course you know already. I never wanted her to be hurt, but I fear it's unavoidable now.'

The room was overheated, to suit Sonia's taste, but Cory suddenly felt icy cold.

She said, 'I don't understand any of this. What are you talking about?'

'About an illusion,' Arnold said heavily. 'An illusion created by a vengeful man and carried out by his grandson. Your lover was bribed, Cory, to set you up. Matt Sansom gave him a loan for that vineyard of his, and then threatened to foreclose unless he managed to seduce you. And I was supposed to pay him to go away. Isn't that the way of it, Mr Rome Sansom? Wasn't that the unholy bargain you made with that old devil?'

Rome stiffened, but his glance didn't waver. 'Yes.'

'No.' Cory's cry of pain and disbelief pierced the room. 'No, Rome, it's not true. It can't be.'

'Yes,' he said steadily. 'It was true, every word of it, in

the beginning. But not any more. Not for a long time. Not after I fell in love with you. You have to believe that.'

'Believe it?' Her voice broke. 'When you've lied to me from the start? When it was just money—all over again? How can I believe anything about you—now?'

She turned away, her body rigid, covering her face with her hands, and Sonia jumped up, placing a protective arm round her.

'Why don't you go?' she hurled at Rome. 'Why don't you just get out?'

Rome turned back to Arnold Grant. 'I'd intended to tell you all this myself tonight, but not in front of Cory. Not like this. You could have spared her.'

'She has the right to know the kind of man you are. The filthy deception you've practised.'

Rome said quietly, 'You can't call me anything I haven't called myself. But it makes no difference, because the deception stopped a long time ago—and my grandfather knows it. I'm still going to marry Cory—with or without your permission.'

'Over my dead body,' Arnold said with a sneer. 'You'll have to look for another heiress to bale out your sinking vineyard.' His smile was thin. 'You gambled heavily on tonight, I think. You'd won my girl. You hope to do the same with me. To use my affection for her to persuade me to trust you. Only the deck was stacked against you in a way you could never have imagined.'

He walked across the room and opened a door. He said curtly, 'You'd better come in now.'

Matt Sansom walked slowly into the room, leaning on a cane.

Rome stood motionless, his attention totally arrested.

Then he said softly, 'So that was how Mr Grant was so well informed. Congratulations, Grandfather. You've actually managed to surprise me. And had your moment of triumph into the bargain.'

Matt looked at him with contempt. 'Did you really think I'd let the fact that you've gone soft spoil that for me? I wanted to see the look on his damned face when I told him I'd offered my bastard grandson money to seduce his precious girl, and I did.' He laughed hoarsely. 'And it was worth every penny I've got to see all his worst fears confirmed.'

Cory said very quietly, 'Why do you hate me so much, Mr Sansom?'

He swung round, looking for the source of the intervention. She was very white, and there were tears glistening on her eyelashes, but she was in control again, standing straight, her head high. Rome's amethyst glittered on her hand and Matt's eyes went straight to it, and then, sharply, to her face.

He gasped harshly and took a step back, his own face blanching. 'That ring,' he said hoarsely. 'Where did you get it?'

'Aunt Kit gave it to me,' Rome said. 'For the woman I love.'

'She had no right.' Matt was ashen, fighting for control. 'I gave that ring to my Elizabeth.'

'And she gave it back,' Rome said quietly. 'When she decided to marry someone else.'

'It was the ring that gave you away,' Arnold said grimly. 'Beth was wearing it when I met her, and I've never forgotten it. As soon as I saw it I guessed who was behind all this.' He sent Matt a look of frank loathing. 'And he was only too happy to confirm it.'

'But he misjudged his man. You can tell who you damn well please about this filthy plot of yours—if you dare— but you'll not see a penny of my money. And you'll never have anything to do with my granddaughter again. She's going to Miami with her mother.'

Rome was looking at Matt, too. He said slowly, 'You gave the ring to your wife—to my grandmother—but she hated it, didn't she? Because she guessed it had belonged to someone else—someone you'd loved in a way you'd never cared for her.'

'There was never anyone else in the world for me.' Matt's voice cracked. He took a step forward, putting out a shaking hand to where Cory stood, pale and straight in her aubergine dress. 'It could be her,' he muttered. 'Her eyes—her gentle mouth. Beth—oh, my Beth...'

'No,' Rome said, his voice like ice. 'My Cory—the girl I love.'

'You dare to say that?' Arnold almost exploded. 'After what you've done. The way you've treated her.'

'I'm not proud of the way I've behaved,' Rome said curtly. 'When I first saw her I was obeying instructions, and I admit it. But after that I was following my heart, because, with her, I put out my hand and touched paradise.'

He threw his head back. 'I agreed to do what my grandfather wanted in order to keep Montedoro, because it was all that mattered to me then. But everything's changed now. Cory changed it. She means more to me than a thousand Montedoros, and she always will, because my life is empty without her.'

He looked at Arnold. 'I came here tonight in good faith, to ask you for her. To announce our engagement. In spite of everything, I still want to do that.'

Matt sank heavily on to a chair. He said, 'Well, you can forget that. It's over—finished with. You'll get nothing from him—and when I'm done with you you'll hardly be able to support yourself, let alone a wife.' He laughed again, the sound grating. 'I'll strip you of everything.

You'll regret the day that you crossed me.' He glared round. 'You'll all be sorry, damn you.'

Cory shook off her mother's restraining hand and walked across the room. She faced Rome.

She said, 'Is this what you were trying to say in the car?'

He met her gaze unflinchingly. 'Yes. But I thought it would be better to confess my real identity to your grandfather first. Try and explain. Only, I was pre-empted.'

Her eyes were grave. Questioning. 'Why didn't you tell me before? In Suffolk, or when we came back?'

He said huskily, 'Ironically, because I was afraid I'd lose you. And I couldn't bear it. Couldn't take the risk. And now I've ruined everything.'

She drew a deep breath. 'And the rest of it—is that true? Can your grandfather really take Montedoro away from you?'

Rome put out a hand and gently brushed a tearstain from her cheek. 'He can try.'

She nodded. Her voice was quiet. 'Do you love me?'

'Cory,' Sonia almost shrieked. 'The guy set you up. Tried to rip off your grandfather. He'll tell you anything because he's broke and you're an heiress. Where's your pride?' Her tone became cajoling. 'Forget him, honey, and walk away. If you don't want to go to Miami, I'll take you to the Bahamas and show you such a good time. In a month, I guarantee you won't give him a second thought.'

Cory's tired mouth smiled faintly. 'Unfortunately, I don't think I'm that shallow.' She looked into Rome's eyes. 'Please answer me.'

'Yes,' he said roughly. 'Yes, I love you, heart of my heart, and I always will. You're part of me, and nothing can change that. And I want to go on my knees and beg you to forgive me. Only that's impossible now. We can never be together, because for the rest of your life you might look at me and wonder if your mother was right.'

'That will never happen anyway.' Arnold spoke roughly. 'Because I'm telling you now that if she dares to go with you—if she even gives you a second glance—I'll change my will and leave the whole lot to charity. She'll get nothing. See how she likes that. And see how long true love lasts at that rate.' And he laughed scornfully, triumphantly.

Sonia shrieked faintly, and fell back on the sofa.

There was a long tingling silence, then Rome took Cory's hands in his. He said softly, almost wonderingly, 'My God, *carissima*. Do you realise what he's just said? He's set us free. They both have. They've taken everything and left us with each other.'

His voice became urgent. 'Leave with me now, my sweetest love. Come with me. Because if you stay, they'll have won.' He looked into her eyes, deeply, gravely. 'These bigoted, greedy, selfish old men will have won. And the precious thing we've been building together will be lost for ever.'

His hands tightened round hers. 'Don't let that happen, *mi amore*. Leave them to their plots, and their hating, and their precious millions. I'll make a life for you, if not at Montedoro then somewhere else. Anywhere as long as it's with you. I'll dig ditches if I have to. Anything.'

Cory's face was suddenly transfigured, her eyes luminous.

He remembered how he'd thought once that she was enclosed in an invisible circle. Now, somehow, he'd stepped over the perimeter, and the circle held him, too. He was at peace as never before, and could have wept with gratitude and relief.

She said, 'Yes, Rome. I'll come with you.' And went

into his arms, simply and directly, lifting her mouth for his kiss.

'Cory,' Sonia moaned. 'You're crazy. Arnold's not kidding—he means it. And don't look to me to bail you out.'

Cory ignored her. She said, 'But, Rome, you mustn't lose Montedoro. You can't. It's your whole life.'

He said, 'Not any more, *carissima*. You've taken its place. But we'll fight together to keep it, if that's what you want.'

Cory turned in his arms to look at them all. There was a militant sparkle in her eyes, and a new crispness in her voice.

'No one's going to take Montedoro,' she said. 'Because my grandmother left me some money and we'll use that to save it—'

'A nest egg,' Arnold interrupted dismissively. 'A drop in the ocean. It won't cover the kind of debt he's in, so pull yourself together, because I wasn't joking.'

'Nor am I,' Cory said. 'The original legacy wasn't that big, I agree, but it's grown in the past year or so.' She looked steadily back at Arnold. 'Remember my amusing little hobby? Well, I didn't just watch share prices. I started investing in the stock market—buying and selling on my own account. I even found I was good at it. And I've certainly made enough to repay the loan on Montedoro. With interest.'

'Cory *mia*.' Rome's voice was husky as he framed her face in his hands. 'I can't take your money. Surely you must see that.'

'It's our money,' she said, and smiled into his eyes. 'For our marriage. Our life. Our children. And you must take it, my love, if you want me, because all my worldly goods go with me. That's the deal. And we're going to make great wine, because you know how.'

Her voice deepened passionately. 'Oh, Rome don't you understand? If you refuse now, then they'll still have won, but in a different way. Their hate will have won, and not our love. Are you really going to let that happen?'

He said very softly, 'My darling—my precious sweet.' He drew her into his arms, resting his cheek against her hair. 'Together we'll make the finest wine in Tuscany. And the loveliest babies.'

'Cory.' Arnold held out a shaking hand. His face was suddenly gaunt—uncertain. 'You can't do this. You haven't thought it through. You can't leave me.'

Cory looked at him. She said sadly, 'You wanted me to hate Rome, but you're the one I'll find it hard to forgive, Gramps. Can you imagine what Gran would have said if she could have heard you threatening me?'

She shook her head. 'You must do as you wish with the money. I don't want to be an heiress. I never did. And with or without it I'm going to have a life with the man I love.

'As for you—' she turned on Matt '—you lost your daughter, and now you're losing your only grandson. Both of you are going to be lonely and miserable, and you deserve it. You've wasted years of your life in hating each other, and in the end hatred's all you'll have left. Because Rome and I are going—leaving you all behind if we have to.'

There was a silence, then Arnold said with difficulty, 'Cory, you're very dear to me, and I can't bear this. Is there any way I can make amends?'

She said gently, 'Not while you hate Matt Sansom more than you love me. Nor while you won't accept my husband.'

Rome spoke, his voice cool and very clear. He said, 'This feud has got to end if you want to see us again—if you want to hold your great-grandchildren. But that's your decision. Because we've made ours.'

He took Cory's hands and lifted them to his lips. *'Mia bella,'* he said softly. 'My lady. My dear love. Let's go home.'

Cory smiled up into his eyes. She said tenderly, 'Together—and for ever.'

They had reached the door when Matt's voice reached them, halting and barely recognisable. He said, 'Rome—boy—is—is it too late?'

And Sonia said miserably, 'Cory, honey…' then trailed off into silence.

Hand in hand, they turned and looked at the three anxious, unhappy faces watching them go.

There was a pause, then Rome said, 'You know where to find us. And we'll be waiting.' He paused, then added softly, 'See you at Montedoro.'

And he and Cory walked together out of the room, and into the hopeful promise of the night.

Modern Romance™
...seduction and
passion guaranteed

Tender Romance™
...love affairs that
last a lifetime

Sensual Romance™
...sassy, sexy and
seductive

Blaze
...sultry days and
steamy nights

Medical Romance™
...medical drama on
the pulse

Historical Romance™
...rich, vivid and
passionate

29 new titles every month.

*With all kinds of Romance for
every kind of mood...*

MILLS & BOON®

Makes any time special™

MAT4

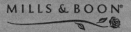

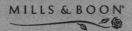

4 FREE

books and a surprise gift!

We would like to take this opportunity to thank you for reading this Mills & Boon® book by offering you the chance to take FOUR more specially selected titles from the Modern Romance™ series absolutely FREE! We're also making this offer to introduce you to the benefits of the Reader Service™—

- ★ FREE home delivery
- ★ FREE gifts and competitions
- ★ FREE monthly Newsletter
- ★ Exclusive Reader Service discounts
- ★ Books available before they're in the shops

Accepting these FREE books and gift places you under no obligation to buy, you may cancel at any time, even after receiving your free shipment. Simply complete your details below and return the entire page to the address below. *You don't even need a stamp!*

YES! Please send me 4 free Modern Romance books and a surprise gift. I understand that unless you hear from me, I will receive 6 superb new titles every month for just £2.49 each, postage and packing free. I am under no obligation to purchase any books and may cancel my subscription at any time. The free books and gift will be mine to keep in any case.

P1ZEA

Ms/Mrs/Miss/Mr ....Initials.....................................
BLOCK CAPITALS PLEASE

Surname ....

Address ....

....

....Postcode.................................

Send this whole page to:
UK: FREEPOST CN81, Croydon, CR9 3WZ
EIRE: PO Box 4546, Kilcock, County Kildare (stamp required)

Offer valid in UK and Eire only and not available to current Reader Service subscribers to this series. We reserve the right to refuse an application and applicants must be aged 18 years or over. Only one application per household. Terms and prices subject to change without notice. Offer expires 30th April 2002. As a result of this application, you may receive offers from other carefully selected companies. If you would prefer not to share in this opportunity please write to The Data Manager at the address above.

Mills & Boon® is a registered trademark owned by Harlequin Mills & Boon Limited.
Modern Romance™ is being used as a trademark.